WITCH

WEED

WITCH
WEED

Phyllis Reynolds Naylor

ILLUSTRATED BY
Joe Burleson

Delacorte Press

Published by
Delacorte Press
Bantam Doubleday Dell Publishing Group, Inc.
666 Fifth Avenue
New York, New York 10103

Library of Congress Cataloging in Publication Data

Naylor, Phyllis Reynolds.
    Witch weed / by Phyllis Reynolds Naylor : illustrated by Joe
Burleson.
        p.   cm.
    Summary: A series of mysterious events and the strange behavior
of a group of their schoolmates convince Lynn and her best friend,
Mouse, that the destructive power of a witch recently killed in a fire
is still very much alive.
    ISBN 0-385-30426-9
    [1. Witchcraft—Fiction.   2. Supernatural—Fiction.]
I. Burleson, Joe, ill.   II. Title.
PZ7.N24W1b   1991
[Fic]—dc20   90-46892   CIP   AC

Manufactured in the United States of America

September 1991

10 9 8 7 6 5 4 3 2 1

RAD

*For Corie Hinton
and her sister, Jaime,
with love*

WITCH
WEED

chapter one

Lynn watched the hands of the clock, but they seemed not to have moved at all since the last time she'd looked. There was no sound in Dr. Long's office except for the shuffle of Lynn's own feet beneath her chair. June 15, read the calendar on his desk.

She had finished the paper-and-pencil test he'd given her—several pages of questions, such as:

I sometimes worry that I will harm a person close to me. Yes or No.

I often find myself crying for no real reason. Yes or No.

Some days I don't want to get out of bed at all. Yes or No.

No, Lynn had written emphatically beside those and many of the others as well. She was *not nuts*.

Then she and Dr. Long had talked about her behavior in the classroom the last few weeks of school, and why she thought the teacher had referred her to him, a school psychologist for the county. Now he was asking what *she* saw as the problem.

"I don't know where to begin," Lynn said at last.

The psychologist smiled. His eyes were blue, as

blue as Marjorie Beasley's new sneakers, Lynn was thinking as she studied him.

"Why don't you just tell me what you want to, not what you think you ought to say," he suggested.

Lynn almost smiled. Surely he could not mean that. The last thing Dr. Long would appreciate hearing was what Lynn wanted to say: that Mrs. Tuggle's witchcraft had affected almost every member of Lynn's family. First it was Judith, her older sister, and then Mrs. Morley, Lynn's mother, who used to have a writing studio in an upstairs room of Mrs. Tuggle's house. Lynn had to say it because it was true.

But Dr. Long would scarcely believe that Mrs. Tuggle had sent nine crows to follow Lynn and her friend Marjorie around once the girls discovered what the old woman was up to, and he *certainly* would not believe that after Mrs. Tuggle's house burned to the ground, with her in it, the evil lived on in her green glass eye, which somehow survived in the rubble.

"It was when my little brother found the eye that everything began happening again," Lynn said at last.

"The *eye*?" the psychologist said quizzically. And then, when Lynn hesitated, he added, "Tell me about it."

So she did. Lynn started with all that had gone on since her family had first become involved with the old woman who used to live on the hill, and then told the part about Stevie.

"Stevie began acting very strange, behaving terribly," she said. "One night when Mom and Dad were out and I was his sitter, I tried to get in his room and it took all my strength to get the door open. Yet there was nothing that I could see behind it. Stevie was on his bed, but his voice sounded different, like he wasn't Stevie at all. He told me to get out."

She stopped, waiting, but Dr. Long was still listening intently, so Lynn went on: "I was scared and angry both. I grabbed Stevie and shook him, and the eye fell out of his pocket. He'd been carrying it around, thinking it was a marble. But once it rolled away, it lost its power over him and he's become the sweet little boy he used to be."

There was a long pause. "What happened then?" the psychologist asked finally.

"I was afraid of the eye, after the way it affected Stevie. So I put it in a tea can and hid it behind a row of my sister's preserves in the basement. That night the whole shelf came crashing down. Then I buried the eye out in the garden, but it kept drawing the family closer and closer to it and making us all quarrel. It was the evil in it, I know. I decided that the only thing to do was to show the evil it couldn't control us, so I carried it around with me all the time. But Mouse said that I—"

"Mouse?"

"Marjorie Beasley, my best friend. That's what we call her. Mouse said that I was different when I was carrying the eye, and then there was the night of the big rain, and a bat got in the house. We heard Mrs. Tuggle's voice calling to us, and I went outside with the eye, following the bat, and was all ready to walk right into Cowden's Creek when Mouse saved me."

"How did she do that?"

"She grabbed the eye from my pocket and flung it as far as she could out into the water. And everything's been back to normal since then, so I don't see any reason why I should have to come here to your office once a week all summer long. I am not nuts."

"I didn't say you were."

"But you think it," Lynn told him. "I can't talk about this to Mom or Judith, because they were both under Mrs. Tuggle's spell once, and I don't want them involved again. Stevie's too young to understand, of course. I've talked about it to Dad, but he only half believes me, I think. The one person I can discuss it with is Mouse because she's seen what went on."

Another pause. "And now this is all over?"

"Yes. No bats, no whispers from Mrs. Tuggle, no quarreling—everything's just like it used to be. Just fine."

"What else is happening in your life right now, Lynn?"

"Well, my sister is teaching me to make freezer jam. As soon as summer vacation starts, I'm going to be sitting my little brother in the mornings while Mom works. She writes books for children. I swim at the Y. Mouse will be going to Ohio to visit her mother, but when she comes back, we'll ride our bikes and go to movies—stuff like that." Lynn lifted the ponytail off the back of her neck to cool herself.

"Any problems getting along with your family or friends?"

"Nope. Not really."

"Any worries? Nightmares?"

"Now that the eye is gone, no."

"Are you being honest with me?"

Lynn looked directly at him. "Yes."

"Okay, then, I'll be honest with you. At this point, I have only four possible explanations for what you've told me. First, that you are a very disturbed young girl who sees and hears things that aren't there. Or, second, that you are a very imaginative person, and have made all this up just to cause a little excitement. The third possibility is that things are indeed happening that we cannot explain, but they have nothing to do with witches. And fourth, that evil *can* live on in a glass eye, and that this is, in fact, a case of witchcraft."

"And which do you think it is?" Lynn asked.

Dr. Long cocked his head. There was a definite twinkle in his eye. "From all I've learned about you, I don't think you are emotionally disturbed or crazy or nuts, as you put it. At the same time, I find it very hard to believe in witchcraft. So my guess is that it's either number two or three." He leaned back in his chair and put his hands behind his head. "Whether you're making this up, or whether things have, in fact, happened as you've described them, I frankly don't know. I try to keep an open mind."

"How can I convince you?"

"Keep telling the truth as you see it, that's all. What I'm going to recommend is that—since the eye is gone and you say that the trouble is over—we discontinue your sessions. Enjoy your summer, as you said. Go places, make new friends. . . ."

"Great!" Lynn said, starting to get up.

"*If* . . ." the doctor added.

Lynn sat back down.

". . . you promise that you will call me if the trouble starts again. I'll need your word on that, and I'm willing to trust you."

"I promise," said Lynn.

"Good." The psychologist took a card from his pocket with his name and office number on one side. On the back, he wrote his home phone number. "If you have *any* indication at all that the trouble is happening again, call me."

"I will," said Lynn.

She bounded from the room with the card in her hand and ran over to Mouse, who was waiting on the bench by the trophy case, her big owlish glasses sliding down her nose, her short straight hair messy from the end of a day at school. She stood up when she saw Lynn.

"Do you have to go to the nut farm?" she asked anxiously.

"I'm free! Free!" Lynn sang happily. "I don't even have to see him again unless I want to. He said to call if the trouble comes back, but otherwise, enjoy the summer! That's exactly what he said!"

Mouse grinned happily. "Do you *really* think it's over, Lynn? That the trouble's gone?" She wanted very much, it seemed, to believe that.

"We haven't heard any more singing or voices, have we?"

Mouse shook her head.

"No crows following us, no cats scratching at the windows, no bats, no songs drifting in our rooms at night. Everyone in my family is back to normal now, and if the evil isn't destroyed, at least it's a long, long way from here. I hope," she added, then wished she hadn't. But it didn't seem to bother Mouse.

"So now I can just think about Mom," Mouse said.

Other than witchcraft, all Marjorie Beasley had talked about for the past few months was how she would be going to Ohio as soon as school was out to visit her mother. Since Mrs. Beasley had left the family almost a year ago, she had not come back even once to visit, and Lynn assumed that Marjorie's parents would eventually divorce. But now Mouse had an invitation to spend two weeks with her mother this summer. At first she had been invited for only one week, then Mrs. Beasley said two, and Lynn had the feeling that if she said, "Stay the whole summer," Mouse would. She had been planning what to take and what to wear for the past few months.

"She'll love my new sneakers," Mouse said as the girls started home. "Blue is her favorite color."

What bothered Lynn was Marjorie's feeling that she had to try very hard to please her mother. As though it was her fault somehow that her mother had left. As though, if Mouse could just make her happy, she might come home again. Lynn hated to see her friend disappointed.

The sky was blue, too, with clouds like cream puffs dotting the wide expanse above the trees, the sun warm on Lynn's arms.

"All we really have to do tomorrow is pick up our report cards," she said. "I'll bet we won't have to do any work at all."

"I hope so," said Mouse. "My bag's all packed, and Dad's driving me to Greyhound at four. The bus gets to Ohio about eight thirty and Mom will meet me."

"You're going to have a wonderful time," Lynn told her, not at all sure, but hoping for the best.

At dinner that evening, Father smiled across the table at Lynn. "Well, how did the first session with 'the shrink' go, since that's what you insist on calling him?"

"What's a shrink?" asked five-year-old Stevie, lining

his green beans up around the edge of his plate and then eating them one at a time.

"A psychologist," Lynn said. "That's what I'm going to be when I'm grown—a psychologist or psychiatrist or something to do with the mind. Anyway, Dr. Long is a very nice man, Dad, and I like him fine."

"Good!" said Lynn's father, and smiled again. It was Mr. Morley whom Lynn resembled, with her long face and light speckled skin like an eggshell. Judith and Stevie, with their widely spaced eyes, looked like Mother.

"Lynn doesn't need a psychologist any more than I do," Judith said. "Just because she's been edgy the last few weeks of school and was a little rude to her teachers doesn't mean she's sick in the head. She's sick of school and so am I. We all need a vacation, if you ask me, and I'm so glad tomorrow's the last day of classes that I feel like shouting."

"So shout," said Lynn.

Judith threw back her head. "Yippeeeee!" she howled, and Stevie joined in. Everyone laughed.

A normal, happy family, right? Lynn told herself.

"Well, I'm really glad to hear that you like Dr. Long so much," Mother said to Lynn. "I'm sure your sessions will be worthwhile. Pass the potatoes, please."

Lynn handed her the bowl. "My first session was my last, Mom. I got along with him so fine that he says I don't have to come back anymore unless I have problems."

Mother paused with her hand on the bowl and exchanged glances with Father. "Was that really Dr. Long's idea, Lynn, or was it yours?"

"His. And I think it's a fine idea!"

"Word for word, Lynn, that's what he said?" Lynn's father kept staring at her.

"I can't remember every *word*, Dad, but that was the way the session ended."

Lynn couldn't help noticing that her mother seemed relieved. "Then that's wonderful, dear," she said. "I think we're *all* looking forward to summer. I've started a new book that is going splendidly. When a manuscript's going well, I feel that nothing can possibly go wrong in the world, but when the writing's difficult, then *nothing* seems to be going right."

"What's this one about, Mom?" asked Judith.

"It's about a plague of grasshoppers that—"

"Don't give the story away!" Lynn cautioned.

Mother put her hand over her mouth and smiled. "All right. I should know better than to talk about a novel before it's done. That sort of takes the steam out of it."

It was Lynn's turn to do the dishes that night, so she rinsed them, stacked them in the dishwasher, and was just scouring the pots and pans when Father came out to get some iced tea.

"You're sure you're telling me everything I should know about your session with Dr. Long?" he asked. "I thought, when we had that conference with your teacher and principal, we agreed you'd see him over the summer. Work things out."

"Not if he doesn't want to see *me*," Lynn said. "Not if there's nothing to work out."

"What are you saying, Lynn?"

Lynn told her father what the psychologist had said about not believing she was seriously disturbed.

Mr. Morley thought for a moment. "Well, sweetheart," he said finally, "if he's not concerned about your mental health, then I'm not going to worry either. How do you feel now? Is all that Mrs. Tuggle business behind you?"

"As far as I can tell, it is," said Lynn. "I expect to enjoy vacation, Dad, beginning tomorrow."

"*That's* my girl!" Father said, and gave her a hug. "If the city goes ahead with that new recreation center they're proposing, there will be more for kids to do around here than let their imaginations run away with them. How do basketball, table tennis, soccer, and gymnastics sound?"

"Sound okay," Lynn told him.

Lynn and Mouse picked up their report cards the next day and Lynn was right—they didn't have to do any work. The teacher finished reading *Hatchet* to them instead—about a boy learning to survive by himself in the wilderness. After school Lynn went home with Marjorie to help with the final packing, including the present Mouse was taking to her mother. It was a tiny bouquet of flowers, made entirely of colored glass, and Mouse had been saving her money to buy it for a long time. Lynn showed her how to wrap some socks around it in the suitcase so it wouldn't get broken.

"Sit in the first seat on the right-hand side of the bus and you'll be able to see the whole road," Lynn told her, as Mouse climbed into the car beside her father for the ride to the Greyhound station.

"See you in two weeks!" Mouse called, and then the car was gone.

Lynn walked back up the hill to her own house and even her footsteps sounded lonely. She spent more time with Marjorie Beasley than she did with her own sister. They often stayed over at each other's home on weekends; they helped out sometimes in Mr. Beasley's bookstore on Saturdays. Through all the terrifying business with Mrs. Tuggle and her witchcraft, they had comforted each other, and now Mouse would be gone until the end of June.

Well, Lynn told herself, maybe it was time to do more things with her own family.

"Stevie," she called when she came into the house. "Want to play 'Chopsticks' with me on the piano?"

"No," Stevie said. "That's no fun."

"What do you want to do? I'll play whatever you want."

"Take me for a ride on your bike?"

"Sure," Lynn told him.

Stevie sat on the seat and held on to Lynn's waist as she pumped her way to the top of the hill, huffing and puffing. All the houses on this street were the big rambling kind, with wraparound porches, bay windows, gables, and turrets. Lynn loved this old Indiana town with its brick sidewalks and the wrought iron fences in front. She loved everything about it except what had happened there over the past year.

"Someone sure is doing a lot of pounding!" Stevie yelled behind her.

"I know," Lynn called over her shoulder. "They're building another house where Mrs. Tuggle's burned down."

She stopped at the top of the hill to catch her breath, and they watched the carpenters sawing and pounding. The outside of the house was done, and men were working on the inside now. It looked a little too much the way Mrs. Tuggle's house used to look, making Lynn uncomfortable.

"Let's go," she said, turning her bike around, and with Stevie holding on behind her, shrieking in delight, they went sailing back down the hill.

When they went into the house later, Judith was playing the piano in the music room, something by Chopin, Lynn decided.

"Help you make dinner, Mom?" Lynn called to her

mother who was sitting cross-legged on the couch, papers spread out around her as she wrote.

"Thanks, dear, but the salad's done and the lasagna's in the oven," Mother said.

Lynn got some lemonade and took it out on the back porch. In preparation for summer, Father had hung a swing from the ceiling, and that, in addition to the old glider, meant that the whole family could sit outside in the evenings. Lynn chose the swing this time, and liked the way the chains squeaked as she moved back and forth. A gentle breeze was blowing, and everything looked quiet and peaceful beyond the yard and the garden. The gate at the back led to the meadow where the buttercups grew, and beyond the meadow was Cowden's Creek.

She found herself shivering suddenly, but it wasn't the lemonade. The last time she had been down that path to the creek, with the wind howling, the rain pelting down, she had sunk in mud up to her ankles as she hypnotically followed the bat.

Lynn closed her eyes now. She would *not* let old memories spoil summer vacation; she refused to think about events that were over. Done with. As soon as Mouse came back from Ohio, in fact, Lynn would suggest that they go down to the creek together, to see it peaceful and quiet in the daytime, so they could erase forever that awful night when Lynn had been lured out into the water and Mouse had saved her by throwing away the witch's eye.

She took another sip of lemonade and leaned back in the swing, pushing her feet against the floor. The late afternoon sun warmed her legs and her lap, and Lynn focused on all the hot, lazy days ahead, when she and Mouse would go to movies, picnic in the meadow, make their own fudge sauce for sundaes, and sit out under the sprinkler.

Her legs and lap went cold suddenly, and even with her eyes closed, Lynn could tell that a shadow had blocked out the sun. Only a moment ago she had seen no clouds at all. She opened her eyes and checked the sky. Something large and gray was moving across it, but it wasn't a cloud.

Lynn stared, goose bumps rising on her arms. It was a flock of birds. Hundreds of them, it seemed— so many that they cast a shadow over the landscape below. Lynn could not quite make out what kind they were. Crows? They came from the north, silently swooping low over the meadow around Cowden's Creek as though flying in formation on orders from an unseen commander. And then, without a sound, they rose into the sky again and disappeared to the south.

chapter two

Lynn set her glass down and walked gingerly back inside the house. Then she ran upstairs, all the way to the third floor—one long room that she shared with Judith, a heavy curtain dividing it into separate bedrooms.

She crouched down at the window on Judith's side, overlooking the meadow, and her eyes scanned the field and creek—back and forth, back and forth. She watched for any sign of movement, listened intently for any whisper, even a *hint* of one of Mrs. Tuggle's songs. There was nothing. The sky, however, had a yellow glow that seemed strange for this hour of the afternoon.

"Dad," she said at dinner. "Do crows migrate?"

"I don't think so. Why? Taking up bird watching? Now *that's* a good hobby, Lynn."

"I just saw a whole flock of huge birds circling the meadow, heading south. I *think* they were crows."

"Well, if they were migrating, they'd probably be going north, don't you think? I'll bet they were geese. Sure you didn't hear any honking?"

"They weren't making any noise at all."

"It happens sometimes—big flocks of birds passing through. If you see any more, call me. I'll tell you what they are."

"I'll bet they were robins," said Stevie. "We colored robins in kindergarten." He turned to Lynn. "Do you know what robins eat, Lynn?" He made a face. "Worms!"

Lynn laughed. But she wasn't laughing inside. The birds she had seen weren't geese and they weren't robins. But yes, she would take up bird watching.

She found herself studying the clock that night, however, not the window. About eight thirty, she knew that the Greyhound bus, with Mouse on it, was pulling into the station in Cincinnati. At eight thirty-five, she imagined Mouse being the first one off, dragging her suitcase with her, looking around for her mom.

Lynn hoped that Mrs. Beasley would be there waiting for her. Hoped she would put out her arms and hug Mouse and tell her how much she'd missed her. At *least* do that much. Lynn could remember last winter when her own mother had seemed withdrawn and distant while she was writing in an upstairs room at Mrs. Tuggle's and had, herself, fallen under the old woman's spell.

It was good having Mother warm and loving again, the way she'd been before, and Lynn wished the same for Mouse. She even wished that Mouse would call her that evening and let her know how things were going. But Mouse didn't call that night, nor the next nor the next.

That weekend, Lynn smelled the scent. She had been lying on her bed on Sunday afternoon, writing in her journal—writing about her session with Dr. Long and how she liked his blue eyes, liked his honesty with her. She wrote how she hoped the long ordeal with evil was over, and listed all the wonderful things she planned to do with her family and with Mouse that summer.

She had just started the next page when she caught a whiff of something. She sniffed the air. It was one of those scents you don't smell every day—a strange kind of perfumy gas—and yet it seemed familiar. Lynn got up and walked around the bedroom sniffing —over to Judith's side and back again. At last she went downstairs and into the living room where her parents and Judith were reading the Sunday paper.

"Anybody smell something strange?" she asked.

"Huh uh," said Judith.

"What does it smell like?" asked her mother.

"Perfume or gas."

"Well, there's a difference," said her father. "Check the pilot light on the stove, Lynn. You always smell a little gas if that goes out."

Lynn went to the kitchen and checked. The pilot light was lit. There was no odor there. She went back upstairs. As soon as she stepped into her room, she smelled it, but then it began to fade, and within a few minutes it was gone. Something coming through the window, perhaps. Lynn finished the page in her journal, put it away, and spent the rest of the afternoon teaching Stevie to play jacks out on the sidewalk.

It seemed odd to actually have to *look* for things to do. When Mouse was around, that was never a problem. They had always celebrated the start of vacation by riding down to the Sweet Shoppe, ordering triple-decker cones, then sitting on the bench outside, seeing which of them could make her cone last the longest without its dripping down her arm. Still, this summer would be a little different and exciting for Lynn because of her part-time job for Mother, and Lynn was looking forward to Monday.

"I want to keep a regular writing schedule, Lynn," Mrs. Morley told her the next morning. "At nine o'clock every day, Monday to Friday, I'm going to sit down at the dining room table and start writing, and work right up to one o'clock. That room is off limits except in an emergency, and I'd appreciate it if you would keep the noise down in the living room as well. Think you can manage this, five days a week, until the end of summer?"

"Sure," Lynn said.

Mother was smiling. "And guess what? Your father's made lodge reservations for all of us at the Dunes State Park the last week of August. We're going to do nothing but lie on the sand, climb the dunes, swim, and eat ice cream."

"Wonderful!" Lynn squealed. The sand dunes on the southeastern side of Lake Michigan were one of her favorite places in Indiana. She grabbed her mother around the waist and hugged her, and Mother hugged back.

"I hope Mouse is having a good time with *her* mother," Lynn said, suddenly remembering her friend.

"I hope so, too," said Mrs. Morley. She gathered up the pages of her manuscript, her research notes, pens, and books, and headed for the dining room.

Lynn picked up an eraser she'd dropped and followed her. "Sometimes I worry that Mouse's mother will ask her to come to Ohio and live with her, and then sometimes I worry she won't."

"Would Marjorie want to go?" Mother asked. "Would she want to leave here? Leave her father?"

"I don't know. She really loves her dad. I guess mostly she'd just like to be asked. She'd like to know she was wanted. Mom, what would make a woman leave her family and move to Ohio, just like that?"

Mrs. Morley spread her things out on the big oak table—lined paper here, scratch paper there, notes, newspaper clippings, reference books, maps, two ballpoint pens, a pencil, an art gum eraser, Kleenex, a glass of water, and a small dish of cherries.

"I doubt that it was 'just like that,' Lynn. My guess

is that Mr. and Mrs. Beasley hadn't been getting along too well for some time before it happened. It may *seem* as though people do things suddenly, but usually it's something they've been thinking about."

Lynn stood at the end of the table, thoughtfully turning her mother's water glass around and around. She caught her mother smiling at her again.

"And I suppose your next question is, would *I* ever leave this family to go off somewhere? Hmmm?"

Lynn smiled back. "Well, would you?"

"I have absolutely no intention of doing any such thing," Mother said. She looked at her watch. "Now. It's four minutes past nine, and I know just how the next chapter should begin, so I'd better get started. Take all phone calls for me, if you're in, and tell them I'll call back after one."

Lynn went to the kitchen where she heard Stevie pouring himself some Rice Krispies. Judith was enrolled in a summer school course, so she had already eaten breakfast, and Father, of course, was at work.

"Well, Stevie, today's my first day on the job," she said. "What shall we do this morning?"

Stevie rested one cheek on his hand. "I don't know. I'm sort of tired. I was awake a long time in the night because of my nose."

"What's the matter with it?" Lynn gave him a spoon.

Her little brother made a face. "It *smells* things. It itches."

Lynn paused and looked at him. "What kind of things? What was the smell like?"

"I don't know what it was. Sort of icky and sort of nice. I had to put my nose in my pillow."

"Well, the next time you smell it, go get Dad and maybe he can find out what it is," Lynn told him. She cleared the breakfast dishes while Stevie ate, and gave herself a good talking to. She was certainly on the verge of letting her imagination run away with her. A flock of birds swooping down over a field and a strange scent were all she had seen and smelled, and there were undoubtedly explanations for both. Maybe it would take a while before she stopped being suspicious of every small thing she couldn't explain.

At one o'clock, when Lynn and Stevie came back from the park, Mother was making tuna salad in the kitchen, and Judith was pouring lemonade for everyone.

"You'll never guess who I sit right behind in Spanish," Judith said dreamily.

"Ken Phillips," Lynn said.

"How did you know?" Judith asked, surprised.

Lynn and her mother looked at each other and burst out laughing. Ken Phillips was all Judith talked about these days.

"Who *else*?" Lynn asked her sister. "Is *that* why you're going to summer school? I can't understand why anyone would want to go to school when it's hot."

"I'm going because I want to get a semester of Spanish out of the way, and the fact that Ken's in my class is positively accidental," Judith told her.

Mother smiled.

"I wish Mouse was back," said Lynn. "Summer just doesn't seem right without her."

"Why don't you ride over to the school this afternoon and see what some of the other girls are doing?" Mrs. Morley suggested. "Marjorie isn't your only friend in the world, you know."

"Maybe I will," Lynn said. It did seem as though she had hardly gone anywhere with any of her other friends lately. For the past year, in fact. She and Mouse had been so wrapped up in all the terrifying things that had been happening up here on the hill that she hadn't wanted to do things with anyone else. But now she remembered what Dr. Long had told her: "Go places. Make new friends. . . ." Okay, she would.

There were only a few small children playing near the front of the school where Lynn and Mouse and the other girls used to play hopscotch, so Lynn rode around behind the building and across the basketball court. Beside the benches in one corner, under the elm tree, some girls had parked their bikes.

Lynn rode over. There were five girls sitting around, their feet up on the bench opposite them. At least three of them had been in Lynn's class—Betty, the tall girl with the red hair; Kirsten, the one with the white-blond eyebrows; and Charlotte Ann. The others were twins from fifth grade.

"Hi," Lynn said, coming to a stop and balancing herself by one hand against the poles of the swings.

The girls stopped talking, and Betty looked over her shoulder at Lynn. Betty was holding the little white rat that she'd brought to school once for a science project. No one said a word.

"Doing anything exciting?" Lynn asked.

The girls looked at each other and smiled a little.

"Maybe," said Kirsten.

Lynn spun her bicycle pedals around, awkwardly keeping her balance against the pole and studying the girls, who were whispering now among themselves.

"I thought maybe we could all do something together," Lynn suggested.

"We're busy," said Charlotte Ann. This time the twins giggled.

"And you don't know the password," said Betty, the white rat perched on her shoulder now. "We're like a club, see."

Lynn shrugged. "Okay," she said. "See you around."

She shoved off and headed back to the sidewalk again, her long ponytail bobbing behind her, ears burning.

*

At dinner that evening, she told what had happened.

"They weren't *nice!*" Stevie said.

"No, they weren't at all," Lynn agreed.

"Well, Lynn, you can hardly expect them to welcome you with open arms when you and Mouse have spent so much time by yourselves. It'll take a while," her father said.

"I didn't expect them to *hug* me," Lynn commented. "All I wanted was to hang around with them."

"Oh, there are a lot of cliques," Judith told her. "Don't let it get to you, Lynn. Find some other people to hang out with."

Mr. Morley passed the bread basket and let Lynn take the largest roll. "Keep trying, honey. Go back in a few days, and I'll bet they'll change their minds."

"Maybe," Lynn said.

Eleven more days, she was thinking, and Mouse would be home. *If* Mouse came home. If she didn't decide to stay in Ohio with her mother. Lynn was almost afraid to look in the mailbox each day for fear there would be a letter from her, saying just that, but the next day passed and the day after that with no word at all.

Actually, the entire first week went more quickly than Lynn had expected, because she was busy thinking up things to entertain Stevie. But when the second week began, with still no letter from Mouse, the time dragged endlessly.

The next Tuesday, when Lynn's sitting job with Stevie was over, she rode to the school again, and the same five girls were gathered in the corner on the benches beneath the elm tree.

This time, when they saw her, however, they got on their bikes and rode off. They didn't even wait till she got near them.

Lynn was surprised to find that there were tears in her eyes. Tears of hurt, anger, and embarrassment. *This* was one of the reasons she wanted to be a psychiatrist when she was grown. To find out *why* people did and said what they did.

Friday came at last, and Lynn called Mr. Beasley to find out what time Mouse would be home.

"The bus gets in about five thirty, Lynn, and I was planning to take Marjorie out to dinner. We should be back at the house around seven. Should I have her call you?"

"Yes, *please!*" Lynn said. "Have you heard from her?"

"Not a word. No news is good news, I guess. She must be having a fine time."

"I hope so," said Lynn.

When the Morleys had finished eating that evening, Mother said, "We're all walking over to the concert in the park, Lynn. Want to come?"

"No. Mouse is coming home. I want to be here," Lynn told her, and was almost glad when everyone had gone and she had the house to herself.

What she had really wanted was to go to the bus station with Mr. Beasley to meet Mouse, but she knew they needed some time together, just the two of them. Seven o'clock came. Seven ten . . . seven seventeen . . . and then the phone rang.

"Lynn?" came Marjorie's voice. "I'm home. Could I come over?"

"Mouse! Yes! Oh, hurry!"

Lynn quickly poured a bowl of Cheetos, Mouse's favorite, a small dish of M&M's, and set them out on the back porch by the glider, along with two glasses of lemonade—sort of a "Welcome" sign for Mouse. Five minutes later she heard the squeaky pedals of Marjorie's bike coming up the hill.

Lynn charged out the front door, down the steps, and almost knocked Mouse off the bike she was so glad to see her.

"Come out on the back porch, I've got all your favorites ready!" she said, half dragging her friend behind her. "I could hardly *wait* for you to get here. It's been the longest two weeks!"

Halfway through the kitchen, she stopped chattering. "Did you have a good time?"

It was then she saw the tears in Marjorie's eyes and heard the little sob, and suddenly Mouse threw her arms around Lynn's neck and bawled.

"Mouse! What's wrong?" Lynn kept patting her shoulder.

"Sh-sh-she didn't ask me to stay, Lynn. She d-didn't even ask me to come back."

"Oh, Mouse!" Lynn swallowed. She hardly knew what to say. "Did she tell you she *didn't* want you to come anymore?"

"N-no, but I thought she'd at least say something about when I could come again. I know it's because she's all mixed up, but . . ."

Lynn grabbed Mouse by the arms and looked straight into her eyes. "It's because she wants you to be where you're happiest, Mouse. And she knows that as much as you miss her, you're probably still happier here than in a strange apartment in Ohio. It's because she *loves* you, Mouse."

Mouse sniffled and wiped her eyes. "That's sort of the way she put it."

"She probably has to wait and see when the best time will be for you to come again. She might just call you sometime and say, 'Come this weekend,' just like that. You never know."

Mouse pulled out a Kleenex and blew her nose.

"Come on, Mouse. Let's celebrate your being home again." Lynn led her out to the screened porch beyond the kitchen. "Tell me everything you did. All the places you went. Did she like that little bouquet of glass flowers? Did it get there in one piece?"

Mouse looked truly woeful. "It got there okay,

Lynn, and she said it was gorgeous. But you know what? On the last day, just after she said how she knew I was happier with my dad than I'd be with her, I accidentally bumped the bookcase, and the bouquet fell off. Two of the flowers and three of the leaves got broken." She sniffled again.

Lynn put an arm around her as they rocked back and forth on the glider. "She'll keep it anyway because it's from you."

"You sure must know a lot about Mom, Lynn," Mouse said, "because that's just what she told me." And then, suddenly, Mouse lifted her head and sat very still.

"What is it, Mouse?"

"I don't know, but I'm feeling really weird. Don't you get it, Lynn? That smell . . . ?"

chapter three

Lynn gave no answer.

"A smell," Mouse repeated. "Now it's gone. No, there it is again. It comes and goes with the breeze. Made me almost woozy for a moment."

Lynn fought hard against the impulse to tell Mouse what she feared. Feared and suspected. But what exactly *did* she suspect? If "the trouble," as Dr. Long put it, came back, she was to call him at once. She had promised. Yet she had not called, so she must not really believe that there was anything worth calling about. Mouse, however, was studying her curiously.

"Yes, I smell it," Lynn said. "That must be what Stevie was complaining about the other day. Probably coming from somewhere outside."

That seemed to satisfy Mouse. It was true, however, Lynn noticed; when there was any breeze at all, the scent grew stronger, and as the breeze died down, so did the smell. When the leaves hung motionless on the trees with nothing to stir them, there was no odor at all. Nothing.

"Now," Lynn said brightly. "Tell me everything you did with your mother."

Mouse settled back on the glider. "Well, after she picked me up at the bus station, we went to this Mexican restaurant, and had a taco salad, and the next day for breakfast, she made waffles. Then we went to a Chinese place for lunch, and—"

"Not everything you *ate*, Mouse," Lynn said, laughing. "What did you *do*?"

Mouse laughed too. "We went to a zoo. We went to three movies. Mom took me bowling, and we went swimming in the pool. She has a nice apartment, Lynn, but it's real small. It doesn't even have a bedroom—just a bed that folds down out of the wall. We both slept in it together. There was hardly room for my clothes in her closet, but we had fun."

Mouse was quiet a moment. "You know what, though? I missed my dad. I hardly even think of him when I'm here, but once I got to Ohio, I thought about him a lot. Every time Mom took me out to dinner, I wondered what he was eating. I thought of him back at the bookstore on Saturday, and wondered who was minding the shop while he went to the bank. I was afraid to call him for fear I'd get *really* homesick. Ohio's a nice place to visit, but . . ." She didn't finish.

"Well, *I'm* glad you don't live there either," Lynn finished for her. "And I'm glad you're back, Mouse, because I missed *you*."

"What did you do while I was gone?"

"I sat Stevie every morning while Mom wrote, but

the rest of the time I moped around. Dad said I ought to go out and make some new friends, so I rode over to the school to see who was there. Betty, Charlotte Ann, and Kirsten were there with some girls from fifth grade."

"What'd you do? Shoot baskets?"

"We didn't do anything. They wouldn't let me join in. Charlotte Ann said I didn't know the password."

"Charlotte Ann said that? She sat behind me all year, Lynn. I thought she was nice."

"So did I. I always liked Betty, too. But they said it was a club. Maybe you have to own a pet or something to belong. Betty was there with her white rat." Lynn thought for a moment. "I don't know why they don't like me. Dad says it's probably because I spent so much time with you all year and didn't do enough with them."

"Maybe if we both ride over there tomorrow they'll take us in," Mouse said. "It could be sort of fun to belong to a club."

"We can try," Lynn said hopefully.

Later that evening, when Lynn and her sister were going to bed, Lynn lay on her side watching Judith's silhouette moving behind the curtain. Judith was doing her nails. Lynn could smell the polish. Could that have been the scent she was smelling earlier? No, she decided; it wasn't that.

"I'll bet it's Wild Raspberry," she said aloud.

"What is?"

"The name of your nail polish. It smells like raspberries and window cleaner."

"It's not. It's Plum Passion," Judith told her.

"Oh. Well, sometime I wish you'd teach Mouse to do her nails. We were in Walgreen's last spring and she saw some cuticle scissors and asked what they were for, only she called them 'coo-tickle' scissors. Her nails are a mess. Worse than mine, even."

"Sure. Bring her up here sometime and I'll give you each a free manicure."

"Mouse misses her mother, Judith," Lynn said, and told about Marjorie's visit to Ohio.

"Well, maybe we could tackle sewing next—just for something to do. I'll teach you both how to make a skirt. How's that?"

"You're wonderful, Judith!" Lynn said happily. "I'm so glad that Mrs. Tuggle didn't . . ."

She stopped suddenly, horrified at what she had almost said. What she had been about to say was that she was glad Mrs. Tuggle hadn't succeeded in making Judith a part of her witches' coven. Mrs. Tuggle had tried. Last summer she had tried very hard, inviting Judith to her house at the top of the hill to learn sewing, she said, but Judith changed in the process. It was only when Lynn interfered, when Lynn broke the spell of the witchcraft the night Judith was about to give Stevie away to the witches, that Judith had recovered.

There was a long silence on the other side of the curtain. "Didn't what?" Judith said at last.

Lynn stared at the ceiling. She had not talked to Judith about Mrs. Tuggle since last summer, never quite sure whether her sister was absolutely free of the power witchcraft seemed to have over her. Lynn had never wanted to remind her of the strange way she had been acting, afraid it might stir up cravings again to dabble in witchcraft.

"Glad that Mrs. Tuggle didn't *what?*" Judith asked again, and came around the curtain, her fingers spread as she waited for the polish to dry.

"Didn't change you," Lynn said lamely.

"*Change* me? How?"

Lynn didn't answer.

Judith came over in her summer pajamas and leaned against Lynn's desk, blowing on her fingernails. "Lynn, do I just imagine it, or is 'Tuggle' a dirty word in this house? Anytime someone mentions her name, there's a silence, and sometimes I catch Dad looking anxiously at Mom. I know that no one likes to talk about the dead, and it's spooky the way Mrs. Tuggle died in the fire, but is there something about her I don't know? I asked Mom once, and all she said was that she's uncomfortable talking about any of it —that she was sick after Mrs. Tuggle died and feels better not bringing it up again."

Lynn simply did not know what to say. She wished she were a psychiatrist already and knew how to answer. Judith had seemed so normal lately—so happy; what if Lynn somehow brought back memories that were better left forgotten?

But *was* it better not to remember things? Even unpleasant, scary things? Lynn decided that if Judith had not asked, had not wanted to know, it wouldn't be wise to bring up the subject. But since her sister had asked, had admitted she'd been wondering about it, wouldn't it be worse not to talk of it at all?

"Tell me everything *you* remember," Lynn said finally.

Judith sat down on Lynn's desk chair. "I remember how Mrs. Tuggle used to call to me sometimes as I went by her house. She seemed friendly—lonely, too —so sometimes I'd go up on her porch and talk. It got so she'd ask me in to have tea, and that seemed so quaint, Lynn! I mean, sitting around holding teacups, eating little cakes off a platter, just like they do in England. It was fun."

Lynn nodded. She remembered the times Mrs. Tuggle had invited her and Mouse in for tea. Spooky, but fun in a strange sort of way.

"She asked me a lot about myself," Judith went on. "Wanted to know if I had any friends, what I liked to do. I told her I wanted to learn to make my own clothes, so she invited me there each night after dinner, and we'd sew."

Lynn sat up and leaned against the wall, knees drawn up to her chest as she listened.

"*Most* of the evenings we'd sew, I guess. Sometimes it seemed we just talked, and sometimes . . ." Judith tipped her head back against the chair. "I don't know, Lynn. The tea started making me feel really weird. Sometimes I'd sit there holding the cup, the steam warming my face, and Mrs. Tuggle would sort of hum some of those songs of hers—recite those strange poems about the bogs of England, the moors, the pools . . . She always wanted me to bring my friends, too. She said . . . I remember now . . . that six girls and one old woman would make a proper tea party. But I could never interest any of my friends in going with me."

Lynn felt shivers run down her arms and back. According to the *Spells and Potions* book in Mr. Beasley's bookshop, it took seven people to form a witches' coven.

"Lynn," said Judith suddenly, looking right at her. "Was Mrs. Tuggle into, you know, witchcraft?"

Lynn was amazed that Judith had made the connection. She took a chance. "I think so," she said.

She was relieved to see that Judith didn't fall over or begin screaming or anything.

"Who all knows this?" Judith asked.

"Dad . . . you . . . me . . . and Mouse. And Dr. Long."

Judith stared. "Do *they* believe that Mrs. Tuggle was a witch?"

"Mouse and I do. Dad isn't sure. He half believes, I think. Dr. Long says he's keeping an open mind."

"And Mom?"

"I just don't know. I think she not only believes but she's still so close to it—to what happened to her at Mrs. Tuggle's—that she can't even talk about it. Not yet. That sort of daze she was in, the cold way she was acting here at home . . . You remember."

"I remember Mom being like that, but did I . . . ?" Judith swallowed. "Did I do anything awful to anyone, Lynn, when *I* was under Mrs. Tuggle's spell?"

Lynn struggled with herself. She wanted very much to tell her—to have everything out in the open between her and Judith. But she decided not to tell how Judith had almost given Stevie to the witches by putting him out on the porch at midnight under a full moon. It was just too terrifying, and might upset her sister very much. Besides, Judith had merely *tried* to do it; she hadn't actually succeeded.

"No," said Lynn. "You might have, but you didn't get the chance."

"I got sick instead?"

"Yes."

"And after I got well—I do remember the fever breaking—I lost interest in going up to Mrs. Tuggle's, and never went back."

"I'm glad, Judith. Glad you're like you used to be."

"So am I. But Lynn, if you ever need me . . . if anything happens again, you can tell me. I don't think I could slip into witchcraft again so easily. Besides, Mrs. Tuggle's gone, so we don't have anything to worry about. Right?"

"Right." *I think*, Lynn added to herself. "Thanks, Judith."

It was the next day, Saturday, that she and Mouse decided to ride over to the playground and see what kind of club Betty and Charlotte Ann had started, and whether or not they could join.

There was no one there at first. A few boys were riding bikes around the basketball court, but no one was playing ball. The benches under the elm tree were empty.

"What do we do now?" Lynn asked.

"We could always sit on a bench and see if anyone shows," Mouse suggested.

So they parked their bikes under the elm tree, swung awhile on a swing, Mouse sitting, Lynn standing. When they tired of that, they sat down on one bench with their feet on another. It was a nice spot. The tree completely shaded the ground below, and Lynn felt a little jealous that Betty and Charlotte Ann had claimed this corner of the playground for themselves.

It wasn't long before Kirsten, with the white-blond eyebrows, showed up. She came riding over, squealing to a stop when she saw who was on the bench.

"What are you doing here?" she asked.

"Sitting," said Lynn.

"Who said you could?"

Lynn stared. "This bench doesn't *belong* to anyone, does it?"

"Us," said Kirsten. "The bench belongs to us. To our club. For the summer, anyway."

"I thought it was 'First come, first get.'"

"Not anymore," said Kirsten and turned her head as another bicycle appeared in the distance. Charlotte Ann rode over. She, too, came to a halt when she saw Lynn and Mouse on the bench, but said nothing.

The clock on the courthouse chimed three, and then the other girls arrived—Betty, with her pet rat, then the fifth-grade twins. They all sat on their bikes in a circle around Lynn and Mouse, not saying a word. Lynn began to feel very uncomfortable. She could tell by the way Mouse rubbed her knees that she was uneasy, too.

Lynn tried again. "Hi," she said, looking around the circle. "Mouse just got back from Ohio. We thought we'd ride over and see what was going on."

The twins looked at Charlotte Ann. Charlotte Ann and Kirsten were looking at Betty.

"Nothing's going on," Betty said. "Nothing, nothing, nothing. That you should know about, anyway."

"Okay," said Mouse bravely. "You want to do something, then? Go downtown for ice cream?"

The twins looked as though they liked the idea, but

Betty just folded her arms across her chest, strad-
dling her green bike and looking off into the trees.

"Well?" said Lynn.

"We've got things to do," Betty told her.

"I thought nothing was going on."

"Not with you, there's not."

"Okay, we get the message," said Lynn, and stood
up. Mouse followed. They got on their bikes and rode
away, the other girls watching.

"Boy, were you ever right!" said Mouse. "If they
were any colder, they'd be frozen stiff. What did we
ever do to *them?*"

"I guess the problem is we didn't do enough. Maybe
we should invite them to a party or something."

"Maybe we should invite them to a party and turn
the hose on them," Mouse said.

They rode to the library and around the downtown
area awhile, waving to Mr. Beasley through the window of the bookshop, and finally heading up the hill
again to the Morleys' back porch. They chose the new
swing this time and sat looking out over the meadow.

"You know what we haven't done?" Lynn said at
last. "We haven't walked down to—"

"Don't, Lynn."

"You don't ever want to go out there?"

"I wouldn't care if we never saw Cowden's Creek
again."

"Not *ever?* Mouse, we used to have fun down by the
creek. Remember how we used to go wading in the

mud along the bank? Make necklaces out of weeds?
Look for lightning bugs? Try to catch grasshoppers?
Lie on the bank and dangle our hands in the water?"

"That was all be*fore*, Lynn."

"But it's over, Mouse! Mrs. Tuggle's gone. If we act
like she's not, like the trouble's beginning again, then
it will. The evil's gone. We've got to start living like we
used to. Why don't we go now—right now—while the
sun's out. Just walk out over the meadow to the creek
and back again. That's all. We don't even have to stop.
The next time will be easier, and the time after that,
and finally we'll forget all about what happened."

"You wish," Mouse said.

"No. Really! Let's do it, Mouse."

"I don't know . . ."

"It'll take ten minutes at the most. Five to get to the
creek and five to get back."

"Let's have something to eat first while we're thinking about it," Mouse suggested.

Lynn went inside and came back out on the porch
with two colas, a box of Ritz crackers, a sack of
marshmallows, and an orange.

"Eat," she said.

Marjorie lined a handful of crackers up on one
thigh, and a handful of marshmallows on the other.
Then she slowly unpeeled the orange.

"It'll be dark by the time you finish all that," Lynn
said.

"Then we'll go tomorrow," Mouse told her.

"Oh, come on, Mouse, while I've got my nerve up. Eat the crackers, and we'll take the rest with us."

Marjorie stuffed the food in her pockets and they went down the back steps, across the yard and garden. The breeze was always stronger beyond the gate.

"See how nice it feels?" Lynn said, spreading her arms, her shirt flapping in the wind.

"It's cold," said Mouse.

"Cool, not cold. It feels wonderful."

Mouse stopped walking suddenly. "There's that smell."

Lynn sniffed the air. "Okay, then, we'll follow it. Find out where it's coming from," she said.

"Lynn . . ."

"Are we going to go our whole lives being afraid because of what happened in this neighborhood once?"

"Yes," Mouse said, but she took a deep breath and plodded on. The clouds overhead swirled menacingly, it seemed, gray clouds rimmed with purple. The girls reached the crest of the hill at last and started down the other side to the creek below. The scent grew stronger still.

"See how purple everything looks along the creek, Lynn!" Mouse said. "It's weird. Are the clouds doing that?"

Lynn studied the landscape below. The ground along Cowden's Creek did look purple. Strangely purple. The girls walked on, and as they got closer, Lynn

could tell that there were purple plants growing along the bank—strange-looking flowers she had never noticed there at all.

"What *are* they, Lynn?" Mouse asked.

"I don't know. But, Mouse, have you ever smelled this smell before?"

Mouse nodded. "I can't remember where, though."

"Me either."

Step by step they made their way down the hill until they were close enough to hear the water trickling in the creek.

Lynn knelt down near one of the purple plants. It was a strange-looking thing—like a short hooded figure. Glancing around, Lynn saw that the flowers were all alike, as though she were surrounded by small hooded monks, heads bent, faces hidden.

"They're really weird, Lynn!" Mouse whispered.

At that moment a wind arose, and as Lynn stared, the hooded flowers raised their heads. A low hum came from within their petals. In unison the flowers turned toward her, as though staring out from beneath their hoods, and long wispy fragments of fog, like bony fingers, swirled up out of the purple plants, scratching the air and clawing their way toward the girls.

Lynn whirled about, and a moment later she and Mouse were racing frantically back up the hill to the safety of the garden.

chapter four

Imagination, Lynn wrote in her journal that night, *can be either a good or horrible thing. I think that because Mouse and I were expecting to find something scary at the creek, we did. Flowers don't hum and fog doesn't claw. Period.*

It was when she went back downstairs to get some grapes that her father said, "I think I saw that flock of birds you were talking about the other day, Lynn. As I left for work this morning, I saw them swoop down over the meadow. You know what I think they were? Gulls."

"Seagulls?"

"I think so. They sure weren't crows."

"I thought gulls lived along the sea."

"They usually do, but sometimes you'll find them in other places. You know about the gulls that saved the pioneers, don't you?"

"No."

Mr. Morley came over and took a couple of Lynn's grapes. "It was out in Utah. A plague of grasshoppers was about to destroy the crops, and gulls swooped in

and ate the grasshoppers. Salt Lake City has a monu-
ment to those gulls."

"Well, I was down at the creek this afternoon and
didn't see any plague of grasshoppers," Lynn said.

"Sometimes birds just appear for no reason. I remember seeing a flock of them circling a parking lot
once." Lynn's father sauntered on into the music
room and played a few tunes on the piano.

Lynn was reassured, though she wasn't sure why. If
Mrs. Tuggle could send crows before, she could send
gulls as well—her way of showing that she could control more than crows and cats. Yet there *wasn't* a
Mrs. Tuggle anymore, and Lynn had to stop acting as
though there was.

Judith was in a sewing mood on Monday. When
she got home from summer school she said, "Lynn,
Lamberts is having a Fourth of July sale, and all their
fabrics are half price. Why don't you and Mouse go
with me, and we'll each buy enough material for a
summer skirt. I'll help you make them."

"I don't wear skirts," Mouse said when Lynn asked
her.

"If you were ever invited to a tearoom with flowers
on the tables, you'd wear a skirt," Lynn told her.
"Make a skirt with Judith and me, and I'll get my
mom to take us to a fancy tearoom."

Lynn was proud of her family, the way they had
circled Mouse with their love ever since she'd come

back from Ohio. Even before, of course. They always tried to make her feel welcome.

"Anytime your father works late at the bookstore, Marjorie, you're invited here for dinner," Mrs. Morley told her once. "In fact, he's welcome here as well. I'll have to invite him sometime."

The material was bought—a blue print for Judith, light green for Lynn, and yellow-checked fabric for Mouse. The girls spent an afternoon and evening cutting the patterns out on the floor of the bedroom, sewing the seams on the old sewing machine in one corner, and adding the waistbands. Lynn and Mouse were sitting on Judith's bed, learning the buttonhole stitch, when there was a light thud, or bump, from below. It seemed to come from the front porch. There was the sound of Mother's footsteps in the first-floor hallway, the squeak of the front door as she opened it. And then . . . the scream.

Dropping the green skirt on the floor, Lynn slid off the bed and galloped down the stairs. Stevie was already ahead of her on the landing. Lynn flew around the corner to the second flight of stairs.

Father had come out of the living room. "What's wrong, Sylvia? What is it?"

Mother stood against the wall, one hand on her cheek, her face gray.

Lynn and Mouse and Judith moved over to the door where she was pointing. There on the doormat was a dead gull, its neck twisted and broken.

While the girls stared, Father went out on the porch in his stocking feet. "Now how on earth did this happen?" He walked to the edge of the porch and looked around, then turned back to his wife. "Don't let this upset you, Sylvia. I'll go get the shovel and bury it out in the field."

Stevie was almost in tears. "What happened to it?"

"I just heard a thump . . . I thought maybe someone had knocked," Mother said, "and when I opened the door . . ."

"Sometimes birds fly off course, get separated from the flock, and fly into things," Father went on, as though trying to reason it out himself.

Mrs. Morley went into the living room and sat down. Stevie cuddled up beside her. The girls followed.

"I've seen that happen at school, Mom," Lynn said quickly. "Remember, Mouse, the day that nuthatch flew against the window in math?"

Marjorie nodded uncertainly.

"Did it die, with its neck twisted like this?" Mother asked.

"Uh . . . I guess not. It was stunned for a while, then it flew away. I guess it depends how hard it hits," Lynn said. "But the gull was probably going awfully fast, Mom. It saw the light and thought it could fly right through." She had no other explanation. "I'm going to help Dad," she said suddenly, and went out on the porch. She could hear her father rummaging about in the tool shed at the back of the house. Mouse came and stood beside her.

"Look, Mouse," Lynn whispered, kneeling down, and the girls stared at the lower half of the door where there was a smear of blood and feathers two feet from the bottom—a long, long way from the window at the top. The bird had not been flying toward the lighted window. Lynn wondered if it had been flying at all. She didn't think so. She felt quite sure it had been thrown.

What kind of person would do such a thing? How could anyone take the life of a bird so cruelly? Lynn guessed the answer before the question had finished forming in her head. Betty, Kirsten, and Charlotte Ann? They would never have done such a thing a few months ago. Could *witchcraft* make you do something you wouldn't do otherwise? Maybe didn't even want to do? Or was it just an excuse to do something terrible, then say, "Witchcraft made me do it"?

"Come on," Judith called from inside. "Let's finish the buttonholes. I'd like to clean up my room tonight."

The girls went back in and let Stevie take their place on the porch, where he was holding an empty box for the gull's burial.

But the trouble wasn't over yet. Fifteen minutes later, just after Father and Stevie had come back inside, the doorbell rang, and this time Father answered. Lynn went to the top of the stairs to listen.

"Why, Mr. Beasley. Come on in," she heard her father say, and Mouse jumped off the bed where she was finishing her buttonhole, and stood beside Lynn.

"Marjorie's here, isn't she?" came Mr. Beasley's deep voice.

"Yes, I think the girls are doing some sewing upstairs."

"I'd feel a little better if she rode home with me tonight," Marjorie's father said. "She can leave her bike here and pick it up tomorrow."

"Certainly. What's the problem?"

"Just some prankster, I think. But I found a dead gull on my porch a little while ago, and I have the feeling someone threw it there. Since I don't know who did it or why, I just thought Marjorie ought to ride home with me."

Lynn rushed downstairs, wanting to stop it all before Mother got even more upset.

"I think I know who did it, Dad," she said. "Those girls from school who won't let us join their club. I think they're just playing tricks."

"Pretty gruesome tricks," said Mr. Beasley. He wasn't smiling. Usually he looked like a big pleasant teddy bear, with his round stomach and the bushy mustache that hung down on both sides of his mouth.

"I know. Mouse and I can't figure out why those girls are acting like this, but we've been talking about it, and thought we'd give a party, invite them over, and clear up the trouble. Don't worry about it."

She could hardly believe the words that were coming out of her own mouth. *Don't worry about it? When her own knees were shaking?*

"Good idea, Lynn!" said her father. "That's the best way to handle these things. Head them off before they get too big. If someone *is* responsible for killing those gulls, we need to put a stop to it quickly." He turned to Mouse. "Well, Marjorie, you ready to go home?"

"I can finish my skirt tomorrow," Mouse said. And then, looking up the stairs toward Judith, "Thanks, Judith. I'll be gorgeous if I ever get invited to a tea party with the queen."

Everyone laughed, even Mother, and Lynn was amazed that Mouse could joke when she was obviously as frightened as anyone.

After Mouse got home with her father, however, Lynn received a phone call.

"What do you think, Lynn?" Mouse whispered.

"I think it's Betty and Charlotte Ann, just like I said."

"Do you think they threw the gulls before or after the birds were dead?"

"I don't know. After they were dead, I hope. Oh, Mouse, I can't stand the thought of someone catching a bird and then . . ."

"Did you really mean it when you said we'd be giving a party?"

"We have to. Dad heard me say it and thinks it's a good idea. We'll send invitations and everything."

"What kind of party? Do we have to wear skirts and drink tea?"

Lynn thought a moment. "How about a badminton party? We can set up the net in the backyard and have lemonade and brownies on the porch."

"Great!" said Mouse, suddenly enthusiastic. "And if nobody comes, we can eat it all ourselves."

When Lynn hung up finally, she realized that she was trembling. She went upstairs and sat down on her bed. Was it time to call Dr. Long? She tried to think what she would say when he asked her what kind of trouble was going on. Seagulls had been seen out over the meadow? Purple flowers were growing along the creek? The flowers were humming? Fog became fingers? *Don't be ridiculous*, she told herself.

But dead gulls appearing at the same time on both her doorstep and the Beasleys' was something quite different. Killing birds at all, any kind of bird, was serious business. If Betty and her crowd were responsible, *how* had the girls caught them? What Lynn could not keep out of her mind was the memory of Judith collecting tadpoles down at the creek when she first came under Mrs. Tuggle's power. The way she crooned to them, and they swam right into her fingers. Perhaps the reason Betty and the others didn't want Lynn and Mouse around was that they had something to hide.

Lynn shook her head. *No.* She was not going to think thoughts like that. Suspecting witchcraft at every turn only helped make it happen. Or *seem* to happen, Dad might say.

I'll give the party, invite the girls, and if they'll admit they threw the birds on our porches, I'll let the matter drop. If not, I'll call Dr. Long, she decided.

On the floor below, Lynn could hear Judith saying good night to Stevie, and then she came up to their third-floor bedroom.

"Mom was really upset about that bird," she said, walking over to sit on the foot of Lynn's bed. "We need something *nice* to happen around here. A party's a good idea, I think. Do you want me to make the invitations? I've got some pretty wrapping paper and I could fold it into little envelopes."

"*Would* you?" Lynn said gratefully. "I'd love it. I was thinking of a badminton party a week from today. Why don't you write 'Badminton Party, Monday, July 10, two to four. Rain date, July 11.' Then add RSVP and our phone number. I'll address them myself."

Judith went over to her side of the room, turned on her radio, and set to work. A half hour later, the beautifully crafted invitations were done. Lynn looked up the addresses in the phone book, stamped the envelopes, and when she took Stevie for a ride on her bike the next morning, mailed them at the corner.

*

It bothered her, however, that when her sitting session with Stevie was over at one o'clock, she heard no lunch preparations going on in the kitchen. One ten, one fifteen . . .

"I'm hungry," Stevie said.

"I'll make some sandwiches," Lynn told him as he followed her out to the kitchen. She got down the peanut butter and the marshmallow sauce, cut an apple into quarters, and poured some juice. With Stevie happily munching out on the glider, Lynn slipped over to the door of the dining room and looked in on Mother, who sat with her chair turned away from the table. She was staring out the window toward Cowden's Creek.

"Mom?" Lynn said softly, hesitantly. "Would you like me to bring you some lunch in there? It's after one."

At first she didn't think that her mother had heard. Then Mrs. Morley turned and got up slowly from the table, as though forcing herself to have lunch.

"I can make my own sandwich, Lynn, don't bother," she said.

It's that gull she's worried about, Lynn thought, and was sure of it when Mother said, "If you find out who threw that bird on our porch, you'll tell me, won't you?"

"Sure. If I find out," said Lynn. Then she told her about the party, and that seemed to perk Mother up,

because she made a sandwich and ate it on the glider
beside Stevie.

Lynn and Mouse didn't go to the playground again
all week, but waited to see if anyone would answer
the invitations. Thursday, Friday, and Saturday came
and went. Nobody called.

"That's not so unusual," Mother said as she and
Lynn baked brownies Sunday evening. "A lot of people think they don't have to answer an invitation unless they can't go. My guess is that all the girls will be
here."

Monday was perfect weather for a badminton
party. Just enough sun to be warm without being hot,
just enough breeze to cool them, but not so windy as
to carry the shuttlecocks away.

Mouse came over with her hair freshly shampooed,
wearing a clean T-shirt, shorts, and sneakers. She volunteered to answer the door when it rang, and Judith
promised to stick around long enough to get the conversation going.

But at two, there was no one there. At two fifteen,
Stevie went out on the sidewalk and looked up and
down the street, but didn't see anyone coming.

"I can't understand such rudeness," said Mother.

"Well, you've done your best to be nice to those
girls, Lynn, and it hasn't worked, so just forget about
them," Judith said. "Have another party sometime
and invite someone else."

"We will," Lynn said determinedly. "Bring on the brownies."

Judith brought out the tray, and the three girls and Stevie ate until they were full.

"I feel better already," said Mouse.

"You know what?" Stevie said. "I've got an idea of something to do, Lynn! Let's take all the old shuttlecocks that don't have any feathers on them and float them down the creek. Remember how we used to do that? Float things? I'd drop them off the bridge and you'd fish them out when they got to the rocks?"

"Sure. Why not?" said Lynn, ignoring Mouse's quick look.

They sorted through the box of shuttlecocks, separating the good ones from the ones that were too old and worn to use. Then, while Judith cleaned up their glasses and put the party things away, Lynn and Mouse and Stevie set out for the garden gate.

Again the wind seemed stronger when they were beyond the protection of trees and fence, and again, as they neared the water, Lynn noticed the raw, perfumy scent of the strange flowers.

Witch weeds, she thought darkly, as she made her way through them.

Stevie ran on ahead to the narrow footbridge that crossed the creek, holding the box of old shuttlecocks under one arm.

"Here comes the first one!" he cried, leaning over

the railing. He held a shuttlecock over the water and let it drop.

The current was moving slowly, so Lynn and Mouse walked along the bank toward the rocks at the bend. They tried to ignore the low hum that came from the purple-hooded flowers; it rose and fell with the breeze.

Lynn climbed out onto the largest rock in the center of the creek, holding a stick in one hand, and fished out the first shuttlecock.

"Here comes another one!" Stevie yelped, and dropped a second from the bridge.

Mouse sat on the bank and watched. "You actually used to play this game a lot?" she asked. "How do you know when it's over?"

"When Stevie gets tired of dropping things," Lynn said.

Mouse rolled her eyes.

Lynn fished out another shuttlecock and another. The hum around her seemed to grow louder. Out of the corner of her eye she saw that the flowers were tilting their heads. The hoods seemed to have become mouths, all hissing at her. She tried desperately to concentrate on the breeze and the sunshine and the gorgeous sky.

Another white tip came floating downstream, and Lynn stuck out her stick to retrieve it, then reached down to lift it out of the water. It was not a shuttlecock. She stared.

There, wet and limp in her hand, was one of the party invitations, unsealed. She looked upstream. Another shuttlecock was coming her way, and another, and then, beyond that, another invitation.

Mouse stood up. "What is it, Lynn?"

Wordlessly, Lynn climbed down off the rock and followed the stepping stones back to the bank. She handed the soggy invitations to Mouse. The others were coming downstream now, one after another, the last three. They bumped gently against the rocks where the rest of the shuttlecocks had lodged.

"Lynn!" Stevie was yelling. "You'd better get them or they'll go around the rocks."

But Lynn was staring at still another white tip, floating just within reach. She reached out with her stick and hauled it in. It was the wing of a seagull, and when Lynn lifted the bird out of the water, she saw that it, too, had a broken neck.

It was too much. Lynn screamed, alarming Stevie, who ran over, and suddenly all three of them were crying.

"Mouse, I just can't stand it," Lynn wept. "How could anyone *do* this?"

"I wanna go home," Stevie sobbed. "I don't like it down here."

Mouse wiped her eyes. "I *hate* them, Lynn, whoever did this!"

"Cowards!" Lynn screamed at the water and whoever—or whatever—might be listening.

They started back up the path through the meadow, Lynn still gulping back tears and holding Stevie's hand. As they neared the crest of the hill, she looked up and there stood Mother.

"Lynn? I thought I heard a scream."

Lynn sniffled. "You did."

"What's wrong?" Mother looked at them curiously.

"Somebody broke another bird!" Stevie told her. "We found it in the water."

Mother paled. "Not another gull? With its neck twisted?" And when the girls nodded, Mother turned away. "It's happening all over again, isn't it, Lynn?" she said.

chapter five

Mother walked swiftly home, Stevie running beside
her.

"What do you think it means, Lynn?" Mouse asked
as the girls plodded along behind.

"I don't know. I don't know anything anymore."

"Call Dr. Long."

"Mouse, think how nuts it would sound! What am I
supposed to tell him? That I gave a party and nobody
came, so it must be witchcraft? That I found the invitations floating in the creek? That I found a dead bird
in the water? I'll wait until there's *real* trouble or he'll
never believe me."

"You might wait too long," Mouse said worriedly. "I
just want to go home and crawl under a blanket and
never come out again. That's what I feel like doing."

"We're going to go right on ignoring all these dumb
things," Lynn said. "We're just not going to let them
bother us. If flowers want to hum, let them hum. If
Betty and Charlotte Ann and the others don't want to
come to a party, okay. I don't know how the bird got
in the creek, and I don't care how the invitations got
there. Betty and the others are trying to get a rise out

of us, and if we ignore them, maybe they'll stop. I just
want to live a normal life."

"You know what's bothering me?" Mouse said at
last. "I was reading some more of *Spells and Potions*
over the weekend, about all the things that witches
can do."

"She's gone, Mouse. Mrs. Tuggle's dead."

"They can curdle milk, start fires, destroy
crops . . ."

"There isn't any more witch, so there can't be any
more witchcraft," Lynn declared stubbornly.

". . . sink ships, and knock birds from the sky."

Lynn suddenly grew quiet. "What do you mean,
'knock'?"

"That's just what it said, Lynn. I read it twice.
'Knock birds from the sky,' it said."

"And you think the two gulls were knocked down
out of the clouds by witchcraft and tossed headfirst
onto our porches, and another one ended up in the
creek?"

"I only know what I read, Lynn."

Mouse went on home, and when Lynn walked into
the house, Stevie had gone up to his room. Mother
was sitting at the table alone, her head in her hands.

Lynn leaned against the refrigerator. "What did
you mean, Mom, about 'it' happening all over again?"

"The things we can't explain."

"You mean the sea gull?"

"Go ahead and say it, Lynn. The family's been protecting me ever since I got mixed up with Mrs. Tuggle. I know it. I can sense it. I see your father's eyes studying me whenever he thinks something's going to remind me of her. I know how delighted you and Stevie are when I'm normal. Tell me the truth, Lynn. Does your father think I am . . . or was . . . mentally ill?"

"Dad doesn't have the answer to all the things that have happened either, Mom. None of us do. But I'm sure he doesn't think you're mentally ill."

"Do you?"

"No."

Mrs. Morley smiled a little. "Cross your heart?"

"And hope to die."

"Don't say that, Lynn."

Lynn smiled herself. "Just cross my heart, then."

"Come here." Mother held out her arms, and Lynn went over. "You're nice to have around," Mother said, and gave her a hug. "Lynn, sweetie, do you think maybe we should go talk to Dr. Long—you and I?"

"We can if you want, Mom, but what would we tell him?"

"Well . . . we could tell him that . . . uh . . . the birds were . . ." Mother sighed, and her shoulders slumped. "There's just nothing to say, I guess, that doesn't sound too ridiculous for words."

*

Judith was going to a movie with Ken Phillips that evening, and Lynn sat by her sister's window, watching as she dressed.

"You look really nice," she said as Judith put on her new summer skirt. "You look good enough to visit the queen of England, as Mom would say."

"If I look good enough for Ken Phillips, that's all I want," Judith told her.

"Have a good time," Lynn called after her as Judith put on her sandals and clattered downstairs.

Lynn didn't want to leave the window. The breeze came in cool and dry, and she had almost got used to the strange scent that came and went from the direction of the meadow. What did she care? What did it hurt? What did it matter?

Something moved in the meadow beyond. Lynn jerked her head. Someone was moving along in the weeds by Cowden's Creek. She leaned forward, resting her arms on the windowsill, chin on her arms, staring hard to see through the dusk. No, there were two people, not one. Three! There were four people . . . *five*, she counted. Five people were moving through the weeds and grass along the creek bank. Betty, Charlotte Ann, Kirsten, and the fifth-grade twins.

Of course. It all made perfect sense. Lynn and Mouse had been so preoccupied during the last year with what was happening in the neighborhood that they had pretty much ignored their other friends at school, and now the other girls were ignoring them in turn. Not only ignoring, but getting even.

They refused to let them join their club. They were so angry, so hurt, Lynn decided, that they found three dead gulls with broken necks, and threw two of them onto the Morleys' and Beasleys' porches, just for spite. When they were invited to a party, they found the perfect way to show Lynn and Mouse just what they thought of them by not coming at all. They were probably nearby all the time, watching the backyard, laughing because the badminton was all set up and nobody came. And finally, when they saw Lynn and Mouse and Stevie heading for the creek, playing that silly little game of dropping shuttlecocks and rescuing them again, they went upstream where they couldn't be seen and floated their invitations in the water, the perfect insult. And then they took the third dead gull and . . . No, it sounded too preposterous, even to Lynn. She had rarely seen gulls around here, and had *never* found a dead one. What were the chances of the girls finding *three* dead gulls, and all with their necks broken?

She sat back against the wall and watched the five girls making their way through the weeds. There was only one answer as to why Betty or Charlotte Ann or Kirsten would take live birds and wring their necks: to keep Lynn and Mouse away. *Scare* them away, so they wouldn't try anymore to see what Betty and the

others were up to. It was what they were up to that
bothered Lynn the most.

Okay, let them have their nasty little club. Judith
was right. There were lots of other girls in town, lots
of other friends at school. The main thing was that
Mrs. Tuggle was dead, the eye was gone, the witchcraft was over, and Lynn could get on with her life.

But it didn't explain the purple-hooded flowers.
This was the point that *really* disturbed her. There
was a familiar scent she could not quite place, and it
most surely came from the direction of the creek.
There *was* a hum. Lynn was not entirely certain it
came from the flowers, but when she was down on
the creek bank, it *seemed* to. The strange plants or
weeds *seemed* to lift their heads, *seemed* to turn in
her direction when the hum got the loudest. *A witch's
weed*, she thought again.

She realized all of a sudden that the girls were gone
—had disappeared into the tall grass on the other side
of Cowden's Creek. Lynn was about to go call Mouse
when she noticed something else. Fog was rolling up
from the creek. In the gloom of early evening, it appeared first like steam rising off the water's surface,
which was just visible from the third-floor window.
But it did not just rise like a blanket. It seemed to
swirl, to dance, and as Lynn watched—too aston-
ished to move—the fog came together and took shape
—lumps of fog, strands of fog, fingers of fog that be-

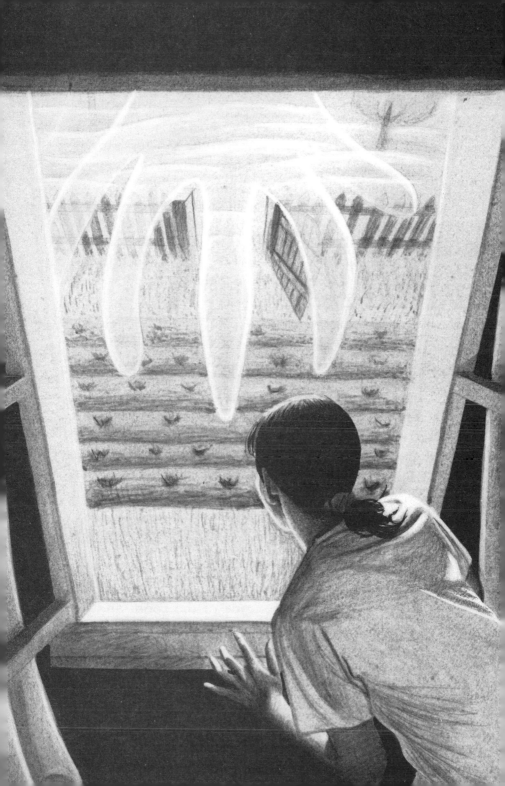

came a hand—a huge white ghost of a hand that came clawing up the hill toward the Morleys'.

Lynn rose to her knees, gripping the windowsill. And then, as she stared, the foglike fingers reached the gate and stopped, as though to unlatch it. The gate swung open, and the hand crawled on across the garden toward the house.

Scrambling across the floor, Lynn struggled to her feet and ran to the top of the stairs.

"Dad!"

"What?" came his voice from the living room.

"Look out the back door!"

She heard his footsteps in the hall, the kitchen. The opening of the back door. Then, from out on the back steps, "What do you want me to see, Lynn?"

Knowing that he was down below, Lynn crept back to the window and peered out. The foggy fingers were gone. The whole backyard was enveloped in mist, as though the hand was covering it completely. What could she possibly say?

Now her father was out in the yard himself, looking up at her. She could just barely make him out. "What'd you see, Lynn?"

"The fog . . ." she said weakly.

"Beautiful, isn't it?" her father said.

Lynn went over to her side of the room and lay down, heart thumping.

*

She did not tell Mouse about the hand when she called the next morning. She told no one, because at this point she was not sure *what* she had seen, or whether she had seen anything at all. People saw all kinds of shapes in clouds; they could do the same with fog.

She did, however, tell Mouse that she had seen the five girls down by Cowden's Creek. Marjorie shrugged it off.

"Let's give another party and invite someone else," Mouse said. "And of course we have to have brownies and lemonade again."

"In a couple of weeks, maybe. I just sort of want to wait until all this blows over."

"Okay then, guess what? Dad's having a sale at the bookstore on Saturday and said he could use some help. And he *also* said that if we'd help out *every* Saturday morning for three hours, he'd pay us a dollar an hour each."

"I'd *love* it!" Lynn said. "What do we have to do?"

"Straighten the books after customers have rummaged through them, clean the glass on the front door, unpack deliveries, dust the shelves—that sort of stuff."

"Great! I don't sit Stevie on Saturdays. And if we're there in the store all morning, maybe we could—" She stopped.

There was silence on the other end of the line. Then, "We could read some more of *Spells and Po-*

tions, right? So we're really *not* over it, are we, Lynn?"

"I just want to make sure," Lynn told her.

On Saturday at the bookstore, while the girls were dusting the shelves, Lynn tried to explain: "I just wanted to see that part you read about witches being able to knock birds out of the sky. To see if it's possible that the gulls could have . . . well, you know . . ."

"Flown into our doors by accident, both at the same time," Mouse finished for her. "It's okay, Lynn. Dad says we can read the books in the display case if we don't take them out of the store. We don't have to sneak *Spells and Potions* out anymore. We get a fifteen-minute break in the middle of the morning, so maybe we can read it then."

"This is *perfect!*" Lynn told her.

Lynn worked hard at the Beasley Book Shop because she wanted Mr. Beasley to feel that she was worth the money he was paying her. She got out the carpet sweeper and ran it over the floor where someone had tracked in dirt. She wiped off the glass again where a child had left fingerprints, picked up a book that had fallen over in the window display, helped a customer find what he wanted in the history section, and stood at the counter bagging purchases when a college literature class came in to look around, and each student bought a book. Mouse, who knew even more about her father's business than Lynn, sat in the little room at the back, opened the mail, and helped look for books that were ordered by phone.

"Okay, gals, take a break," Mr. Beasley said at ten thirty. "If you want a Coke, there's a machine outside. Just don't eat or drink anything in the store."

"We just want to look at books," Mouse told him, and carefully took *Spells and Potions* out of the case behind the cash register. Then she and Lynn squeezed into the big easy chair in the storeroom.

"First the section about knocking birds out of the sky," Lynn said, and was glad that Mouse had already left a small slip of paper between the pages so they could find it easily.

EVIL EYE, the heading read.

> *One of the most feared of a witch's powers is that of the evil eye. The destruction that a witch may cause may be so small as to be merely mischievous in a household, or so large as to cause great suffering for an entire village. In the former instance, clothing may be torn, milk soured, food spilled, jewelry rent, or household items displaced. When a town is affected, cows may dry up, corn may wither, and birds in flight may be knocked from the sky. There have even been reports of great waves being cast at sea and ships sunk in harbour, so great is the charm of a witch's eye.*

"It doesn't prove anything one way or another, does it?" Lynn said, reading the paragraph a second time. "Boy, I wish this book had an index. Mouse, can you remember reading anything at all in here about weeds or flowers?"

Mouse carefully turned the pages. "I'm not sure. Why don't we start at the beginning, and every time we come to something we think we might need, we'll put in a slip of paper."

"Do you realize how many pages are in this book? If we read two or three a day, every Saturday, it will take us years!"

"Do you have a better idea?"

"No."

"Then start tearing up little strips of paper," Mouse said.

The worst thing about the book, next to its being so old that the edges of the paper were crumbling and the girls had to turn them very, very carefully, was that the sections weren't even alphabetically arranged.

SABBAT, the book began, when you would think the *S*s would be near the end.

> *It is one of the curiosities of witchcraft that there are celebrations known to witches as their Sabbat, a time at which witches gather to converse, to dance, and to plan more mischief with their evil powers. There are four great Sabbats which occur each year, and though these may vary from coven to coven, they are most likely to be February 2 (Candlemas), the Eve of May 1*

(Walpurgis Night), August 1 (Lammas), and October 31 (Halloween). . . .

"Customers," came Mr. Beasley's voice from the doorway of the storeroom.

The girls got up, carefully closed the book, and returned it to its place in the rare book case before they started work again.

It was that evening, just after dinner, when Lynn had gone over to Judith's side of the bedroom to open the window wider, that she saw the five girls again out in the field along the creek. This time they were standing in a circle.

She ran downstairs and phoned Mouse. "Come over," she whispered.

"I'm right in the middle of dessert. Cherry pie."

"Eat it on the way, Mouse! Come over!"

"It's cherry pie à la mode! Have you ever eaten cherry pie à la mode on a bicycle?"

"Mouse, this is important! Just stuff it in your mouth and come! I'll meet you out in the yard."

It was only a few minutes later that Mouse arrived, and she had cherry pie all around her mouth. "What's the big hurry? Did you find another seagull?"

"No. But I saw Betty and Kirsten and the others out in the field again along the creek. They didn't just follow us that one day and float their invitations downstream, Mouse. I have the feeling they've been out there before. Holding their club meetings there, maybe."

"So what?"

"Aren't you *curious*?"

"Lynn, what's so unusual about playing along the creek? We used to go out there all the time before—" She stopped.

"Okay. *I'm* curious, then. *I* want to know what they're doing."

Mouse pulled a Kleenex out of her jeans and wiped off her mouth and fingers. "It's you who won't let it rest, Lynn. 'Just go on living our lives,' you said. 'Just act like nothing's wrong. If we go on believing in Mrs. Tuggle's witchcraft, then things *will* happen,' you said. I was perfectly content to sit home and finish my cherry pie, but *you* wanted to go spying. I didn't even get to the ice cream. . . ."

"Okay, Mouse. Go home and finish your pie."

Mouse looked as though she was considering it. "What will *you* do?"

"Go by myself."

"Oh, no, you won't. You know what happened the last time you set out for the creek alone."

"Come with me, then."

The problem was how to get down to the water without the other girls seeing. The path directly behind the Morleys' house, from the back gate to the footbridge, went through low-lying grass. Lynn and Mouse had to go the long way around, through shrubs and trees that grew on the hill, until they came down by another path where, behind a clump of blueberry bushes, they could see the five girls sitting in a circle below, sitting so that their knees were touching. The scent of the purple flowers filled Lynn's nostrils.

There was a candle burning in the middle of the circle, and the weird thing was that the girls seemed to be chanting in a language that Lynn couldn't understand—just a bunch of nonsense words. Betty would say them first, then the girls would repeat them: *"Bathim pursan abigar shaddar; asmon loray valefar marbos pruslos. . . ."* Sometimes they even talked to the rat, who scurried about in a little cage Betty had brought with her. On and on the chanting went, and Lynn realized they were saying the same words over and over again.

"This is all so stupid," Mouse whispered. "I'm glad they *didn't* let us join. Can you imagine coming down here every evening, Lynn, to sit around a candle and recite gibberish? I thought maybe it was an adventure club, or book club, or bicycle club or something."

Lynn didn't answer because she noticed something else. And as the chanting continued and Mouse grew silent, Lynn was sure that she had noticed, too. It was not just the four other girls who were answering Betty: It was the crows as well. High in the branches of a tree above Cowden's Creek, a flock of crows sat motionless, watching. They made no sound at all when Betty was talking, but when the other four girls answered, they cackled and cawed. Eventually they were joined by several gulls, circling above, so that whenever the cawing began, the gulls added shrieks and screeches.

Lynn and Mouse looked warily at each other. And then they heard the chanting stop. There was a long pause that made Lynn wonder whether the girls knew they were there listening, whether the birds, somehow, had given them away. Then each girl held her hands over the candle in turn, afterward touching her fingers to her eyes and ears and lips.

"August first," Betty said, looking around the circle. "August first, otherwise known as Lammas, is the next of the great Sabbats. . . ."

And every inch of Lynn's body went cold.

chapter six

At first Lynn thought that Mouse had grabbed her arm, and then she realized that the fingernails digging into her skin were her own.

Easy, she told herself. *Just take it easy.* The girls could still be "playing" at witchcraft. Just fooling around—something to do to pass the long, hot days of summer. She knew that. She knew that girls and boys often had silly clubs, and remembered when she belonged to a "magic" club back in fourth grade, and they all pretended they were magicians. In third grade it was a "drawing" club. Every Saturday, a group got together and drew pictures. Was it really so unthinkable that five bored girls might decide to form a club over summer vacation and pretend they were witches?

No matter how Lynn tried, she could not make her lips say *No* . . . no, it was not unthinkable. *Yes*, she thought. Yes, because why here, where Mouse had thrown the eye? Why now, when strange things had been happening lately that Lynn could not explain?

She felt Mouse nudge her shoulder, and glanced at her frightened face.

Let's go, Marjorie mouthed.

Lynn agreed. They were too close, too dangerously close, to whatever was happening. And while Betty talked on, Lynn and Mouse moved backward in the bushes, inch by inch, until they couldn't see the five girls anymore, couldn't hear Betty's voice, and then they stood up and broke into a run. They did not stop until they were far away. Then they leaned against a fence, sides aching.

"Is this it, Lynn?" Mouse panted. "*Now* is it time to call your psychologist and tell him what's going on?"

"Maybe." Lynn waited until she caught her own breath. "Or maybe I just won't get involved. Maybe that's what they *want*, you know? To make us so curious about what they're up to that we'll just beg to join their club. Maybe it's all planned to be so secret that we'll go crazy with wanting to be a part of it, so that no matter *what* kind of club it turned out to be— potholder makers or bug collectors—we'd ask if they'd please, please, take us in."

"Except that you don't believe that at all. You believe they *are* witches, Lynn. Witches-to-be, anyway."

Lynn nodded. "Yes," she said finally. "That's what I think they are, or want to be."

"Then . . . ?"

"Then they can get along fine without me."

The roundabout path they had taken was closer to the Beasleys' house than the Morleys', so the girls ended up there for a while. Once inside, Mouse opened the refrigerator and solemnly took out milk and lunch meat and cheese and strawberries. Lynn couldn't help staring. If Mouse were facing a firing squad, she would actually ask for a last meal.

"Helps me think," Mouse said, in response to Lynn's stare.

Lynn sat down across from her, but she wasn't hungry. "I've changed my mind," she said. "I *do* want to know what those girls are up to. If we could listen in a few times, we might make sense of everything that's been happening, and wouldn't have to worry."

"Uh-uh." Mouse held up a large, plump strawberry by the stem and dropped it with a *whop* into her mouth. "If the sun were always shining and the birds were always singing and everyone were kind to everyone else and nobody ever got sick or died, you would *still* worry. I know you, Lynn. Is this the way we're going to spend our summer? Crawling through weeds every day to listen to girls chant?"

"Till we learn something, yes. Until we figure out if this is all make-believe or whether they can really cause things to happen. And if it *is* something to worry about, I'll have something definite to tell Dr. Long—not just stuff that sounds too dumb to believe."

Mouse sighed and studied a note taped to the refrigerator: *Marjorie, please put the meat loaf in at six, along with the potatoes. We'll eat at seven.*

"Late supper tonight," Mouse said, glancing at the clock.

"I'd better go," Lynn told her. "See you."

When she got inside her own house, her family was well into the evening meal.

"Sorry," she said, sliding into her chair. "I was out with Mouse and lost track of the time."

"Making any new friends?" Father asked. "You and Marjorie getting around some?"

"Well, we're trying," Lynn said, which wasn't exactly the truth.

"Good," said Father. He always pronounced it as though that were the end to the conversation. As though, once he said "good," that put a stamp of approval on the day, and everyone could go to sleep without a care. If only life were that simple.

For the next few days, it seemed as though Lynn and Mouse either just missed the girls after they'd met by the creek, or were there too early and gave up before they came.

"We've got to get there sooner and stay longer," Lynn said. "Let's start out tomorrow afternoon at three."

When Mouse came over the next day, she was wearing a hunting cap with a long bill in front, and carrying a large magnifying glass. As Lynn came down the front steps, Mouse said, "Secret Agent M, reporting for work, sir."

"Don't be ridiculous," said Lynn.

"If I'm not ridiculous, my knees would knock so hard I'd fall down," Mouse replied.

They made their way over the long roundabout path leading to the creek, but what neither girl realized, until they were almost to the clump of blueberry bushes, was that storm clouds were gathering overhead.

"This is plain dumb, Lynn," Mouse said at last when she noticed them. "We're going to be drenched."

"If there's no meeting, we'll go home. If there *is* a meeting, those girls will be drenched along with us. We've got to be quiet, now. From here on, don't make a sound."

They crept forward on the far side of the blueberry bushes away from the creek. When they got to the small open space where they could see the bank below, however, there were the five girls, standing in a circle this time, each stretching her arms up toward the sky. Again they were chanting: "*Bathim pursan abigar shaddar; asmon loray valefar marbos pruslos. . . .*" This time, Lynn remembered that she had heard those words before. So did Mouse.

"Mrs. Tuggle!" Mouse whispered. "When she called the crows . . . !"

Lynn nodded grimly. It was the time she and Mouse had hidden here behind the blueberry bushes, just as they were doing now. And Mrs. Tuggle, her long gray hair loose and streaming down her back, had lifted her arms toward the sky, and the nine crows—the same that had followed Lynn and Mouse around—had come swooping down to light on the old woman's outstretched arms. Once or twice it looked as though a crow or gull was about to come down into the circle now, but then it flew off.

And then the rain came. Big drops at first, like the splatter from a leaky faucet. Then more drops, faster and faster, and before Lynn had time to think, she saw the five girls look up the path where she and Mouse were hiding.

"Mouse!" she whispered, grabbing the band of Marjorie's shorts and pulling her even deeper into the tangle of bushes, branches scratching their faces and arms. "They're going to come up here."

A zigzag of lightning slashed the sky, a clap of thunder startled the birds, and then the rain came pelting down.

"Hurry, Kirsten!" came Betty's voice.

"I've got the candle!" yelled one of the fifth-grade twins. And the five girls came scrambling up the steep path, their sneakers flying past the place where Lynn and Mouse crouched.

Lynn did not move until she was sure they were gone. It was another minute before she convinced Mouse that the path was clear. They ran, taking the shorter path straight up to the Morleys' this time, their hair matted, cheeks cut by brambles, jeans covered with burrs and berry stains, both of them drenched to the skin.

Up in Lynn's bedroom, the girls stood at the window, sharing a towel and looking out over the meadow where the long grass was jiggling under the pelting rain.

"Where did they *learn* all that?" Mouse asked. "How did they *know*?"

Lynn shook her head. "It gets worse and worse, doesn't it? Mouse, did you ever see *any* of them going to Mrs. Tuggle's when she was alive? I didn't. How could she have taught them anything?"

Marjorie's face was pale, and without even asking, Lynn knew they were both thinking the same thing.

"The eye?" Mouse said, fearfully.

"It *must* be. Wherever it is, it left evil behind. In the water, maybe. Spores of evil, that washed up on the bank. That's what the flowers are, I'm convinced of it. Mrs. Tuggle's evil."

"Oh, Lynn!"

"That's got to be what's happened to Betty and the others. They used to be nice, Mouse. They used to play down by the creek all the time, just like we did. But this time, the evil was there."

"Lynn," Mouse said earnestly, pushing the wet strands of hair from her face, "let's just have a normal life, and spend the rest of the summer eating ice cream. Let's go back to school fat. Let's get so fat no one will recognize us and will leave us alone. Okay? Okay, Lynn? Just a normal life?"

"Okay," said Lynn. But they both knew she didn't mean it.

What happened on Saturday was entirely unexpected. Lynn and Mouse went to Mr. Beasley's bookstore as usual. They straightened the books and dusted the shelves, checked in a United Parcel order, answered the phone, cleaned the rest room, put more paper towels in the dispenser, and took over the cash register when Mr. Beasley left for the bank about eleven with the week's earnings. It was while he was gone that it happened.

There were no customers in the store, so Mouse unlocked the display case behind the cash register and took out the fragile copy of *Spells and Potions*.

"Flowers," said Lynn. "We want to see if the book says anything at all about purple-hooded plants."

"I don't know how long it will take to find out," Mouse said. "We agreed to start at the beginning, remember, and read straight through. Here's where we left off last time. The next section is *'Familiar.'* "

"What's familiar?"

"That's the name of it, Lynn. *'A witch's familiar,'* it says, *'is her helper, which takes the form of a goat, a bat, a bird, a dog, a cat, or any number of other creatures.'* "

"Like Betty's white rat?"

"Maybe."

"What's the section after that?"

" 'Nightshade and Other Poisons,' " Mouse told her.

"Maybe it's in there—purple-hooded flowers," Lynn said.

But Mouse was still thumbing gently through the pages, and suddenly she stopped and stared.

"What did you find?" Lynn asked, leaning over. She looked where Mouse was pointing. BATHIM, it read under the section on demons. Her eyes followed the line.

> Bathim, Pursan, Abigar, Shaddar, Asmon, Loray, Valefar, Marbos, and Pruslos are the nine Great Subordinate demons controlled by the Six Superior Spirits which are, in turn, under the command of Lucifer, Beelzebub, and Astorath. A witch may vastly increase her powers if she can learn to dominate a demon by force of will. If she succeeds in sacrificing a subordinate demon, she may win the favor of the Six Superior Spirits. And if she can bring herself to sacrifice her familiar, she will gain the recognition of one of the Three Infernal Spirits Supreme, and hence attain her greatest power.

The girls looked at each other in horror.

"The seagulls," Lynn said. "The dead gulls on our porches. They weren't just killed to annoy us, Mouse. They were sacrificed, *then* tossed on our porches."

"Oh, Lordy!" Mouse exclaimed.

Lynn leaned over the book again to see if it told how to recognize a demon and, once you did, to catch it and sacrifice it. She wanted to know how Betty and the others had managed. Just then the bell on the shop door tinkled.

"Customers," said Mouse, starting to close the book, and then she stared as Charlotte Ann, Betty, Kirsten, and the fifth-grade twins entered the store.

Mouse stood frozen behind the counter. Lynn didn't move either, just watched as the girls came over and stood in front of them, Betty leading the way.

"We came to buy a book," said Betty.

"Which book?" asked Mouse.

"That one," said Charlotte Ann, pointing to *Spells and Potions.*

Lynn could hear Mouse swallow.

"It's a very rare book," Mouse told them. "There're only a few copies left in the world, so I can't sell it."

"What do you mean, you can't sell it?" Betty asked. "This is a store, isn't it? You sell books, don't you?"

"Yes, but this one costs a lot of money."

"Well, we want to buy it," said Betty. She reached in the pocket of her shorts and took out a credit card, placing it on the counter. "How much is it?"

Mouse looked helplessly at Lynn.

"Why do you want it?" Lynn asked the girls.

"What difference does it make?" Betty's eyes grew

darker. "You aren't supposed to ask customers why they want a book. You're just supposed to sell it."

"Well, we aren't," Mouse told them. "Only Dad can sell books from the rare book case. We'd have to get his permission."

"So ask him," said Charlotte Ann.

"He's out at the moment."

"We'll wait," said Betty. "In the meantime, let us see it."

Lynn put one hand on the book and held on tightly. "Not until Mr. Beasley comes back."

"What kind of a bookstore *is* this?" snapped Kirsten, the skin above her white-blond eyebrows pink with anger. "Give us the *book!*" She put her hand on the other side of it.

Lynn knew she did not dare hold on. Already one copy of this rare book had been destroyed, and any kind of tugging or pulling would tear the fragile pages from their binding. She could not be responsible for losing one of the few remaining copies. But could she possibly let the girls have it, even for a couple of minutes? What if they ran out of the store with it? What if they killed something else? If they were willing to sacrifice seagulls, what would it be next time?

"Dad!" Mouse said suddenly, and when the girls turned toward the door, Mouse whisked *Spells and Potions* off the counter and onto a shelf beneath. There was no one at the door.

The five girls made a semicircle around the counter.

"Give us the *book!*" Betty demanded, her jaw tightening.

"The book!" Charlotte Ann repeated.

"The book, the book, the book . . ." chanted Kirsten and the fifth-grade twins. They moved in closer still, and Betty took a step behind the counter.

"Dad!" Mouse said again, and this time Mr. Beasley appeared in the doorway. The five girls moved back.

"What's the problem?" he asked, coming over.

"They want to buy *Spells and Potions,*" Mouse told him.

Mr. Beasley adjusted his glasses and looked at the five girls.

"*Buy* it?" he said to Betty. "I thought you got all you needed from it for your summer school report."

Lynn's mouth fell open. Betty and the others had been coming to the shop, then, and Mr. Beasley had allowed them to *look* at it? The five girls weren't even *going* to summer school. She saw the shock in Marjorie's face as well.

"Not quite," Betty answered. "And now we want to buy it."

"This is a very rare book, girls," Mr. Beasley said. "I couldn't sell it for less than two thousand dollars." He smiled. "You may well find all you need to know at the public library. Ever think of that?"

"We don't want library books, we want this one," Charlotte Ann said.

And again, Betty tapped the edge of the credit card impatiently against the countertop.

Lynn felt as though everything she had ever feared was coming to pass. She could not imagine anything worse than Betty and Charlotte Ann and their crowd getting possession of *Spells and Potions.* What they might already have learned was terrifying enough. But what could she do? If Betty could pay for it, how could Mr. Beasley refuse to sell it?

"Whose credit card is this?" Mr. Beasley asked.

"My father's," said Betty. "We have his permission. He collects books himself, and he'll add it to his collection when we're done."

Lynn could see no hope in stopping them. And then Mouse saved the day.

"We can't sell that, Dad. A woman called earlier and asked me to hold it for her."

Mr. Beasley looked at Mouse. "Who was it?"

"I—I don't know. Someone from a . . . a college, I think. She wants to come by and see it, and I said we'd hold it for her."

"Well, then, girls," Mr. Beasley said, turning back to Betty, Charlotte Ann, and Kirsten. "If you're still interested, stop by in a few days and we'll see if this woman has come in. If not, I'll call your father and talk to him about the price of the book."

Charlotte Ann didn't move. Betty did not move. The

five girls stared hard at Lynn and Mouse for a moment or two, the twins positively glaring, and then they turned and left the store.

"Marjorie!" said Mr. Beasley sternly. "Whenever someone calls and asks you to hold a book—*especially* a book from the rare book case—for heaven's sake, get the person's name and phone number. If she doesn't come by in a day or two, I won't know whether to sell *Spells and Potions* or not."

"*No*, Dad!" Mouse grabbed his arm. "You *can't*, no matter what! There wasn't any woman! Nobody called. But horrible things are going to happen if you sell this book to Betty and Charlotte Ann. If you even let them *see* it again!"

"What are you talking about, Marjorie?"

"Mr. Beasley, please!" Lynn grabbed his other arm. "You can't let those girls have this book, even if Betty's father says she can buy it. We think they're starting a witches' coven. We think they're the ones who killed the birds. We think that Mrs. Tuggle . . . that her eye . . . that . . ." She fell silent. Everything sounded so ridiculous.

"Please promise that you won't sell it, Dad. Not to them," Mouse begged.

Mr. Beasley's body slumped in exasperation. "I won't sell the book to *any*one until I figure out what's going on, but you two are the limit! Some days, Marjorie—and this is one of them—you drive me up the wall."

Mouse was going to have lunch with her father, and so, when the morning's work was over, Lynn rode her bike back home. She still felt shaky. She was relieved that Mr. Beasley would not sell *Spells and Potions*—not yet, anyway—but this did not stop the worry. So now the five girls wanted the book! They had, in fact, already been studying it! All Lynn could think about was that the book was no longer safe, not even behind the locked doors of the display case.

She didn't hear from Mouse all day and didn't try to call her. Lynn imagined that Mouse and her father had had a long talk over lunch, and that perhaps Marjorie had stayed around the bookstore that afternoon also. Besides, what was there to say? What was there to do? *Call Dr. Long*, she decided, as soon as she had proof.

Judith went out with Ken Phillips that evening, Mother had taken Stevie with her to visit a neighbor, and Mr. Morley was reading a magazine in the living room. Lynn had just got herself a saucer of graham crackers and a glass of milk and was taking them upstairs when the doorbell rang. She paused on the landing to the second floor as her father answered.

"Ed!" she heard him say. "Come in! You looking for Marjorie?"

"No, Marjorie's at home," came Mr. Beasley's deep voice. "I wondered if you and I could talk a few minutes, Richard. I'm concerned about our girls."

"Certainly. Let's sit down in here. What are they up to now?"

There was the sound of their footsteps moving across the hall, then the rug, and finally the squeak of the sofa springs in the living room.

Lynn went down a few steps, her ear to the wall.

"I was never sure what really went on with that Tuggle woman—all that business last spring—her house burning down and all," Mr. Beasley began. "I just know that Marjorie seemed unusually upset about it, but . . . with her mother leaving . . . I suppose almost anything at all could upset her."

"I would think so," Lynn's father said.

"As you know, I guess, she and Lynn have been helping me out in the bookstore on Saturday mornings. They've had this . . . interest . . . in a rare book I own, *Spells and Potions*, an old nineteenth-century treatise on witchcraft and signs, I guess it is —and it hasn't bothered me particularly. Some other girls have come by recently, wanting to see the book, too, and I let them, as long as they were careful with it. You know how girls are. They get their minds on something for a while, and then it blows over and they're on to other things. I figured it had something to do with being eleven, interested in witches and all. But this morning . . ."

There was a long pause. Lynn wondered what her father was thinking. Was he nodding? Frowning?

Mr. Beasley went on: "This morning, this same group of girls came into the store wanting to buy the

book on a father's credit card. That's a fifteen-hun-
dred-dollar book, Richard—possibly two thousand—
and I doubt very much that they actually had his permission. If he was a rare book collector, as they said,
he would have wanted to examine the book himself,
and in any case I wouldn't have sold it to them without phoning him first. But what concerns me is that
Marjorie was terribly upset. First she told me she had
already promised the book to another customer, and
then, when the girls left, admitted she hadn't. Both
she and Lynn begged me—*pleaded*, actually—not to
let the other girls have it. If I did, Marjorie said, horrible things would happen. Something to do with the
dead gulls. Have you any idea what's going on?"

There was no sound at all from the living room.
Lynn wondered if the two men had lowered their
voices to a whisper. If they had suddenly been struck
dumb by witchcraft. And then, finally, she heard a
loud sigh, and her father's voice:

"No, I don't, Ed. There have been things happening
for some time now that have been bothering me, too
—things that simply don't add up. But I'd hoped it
was over. I'd hoped that with the death of Elnora Tuggle, somehow our daughters' lives would get back to
normal, and Lynn and Marjorie would have a care-
free summer—the way it's supposed to be for a kid.
I'm really disturbed by what you've told me. . . ."

chapter seven

Lynn kept one hand around the mouthpiece of the phone on the second floor.

"Mouse!" she whispered.

"Lynn, is that you? I can hardly hear you."

"I don't want Dad to know I called. Just a minute . . ." Lynn pulled the phone and its cord around the corner and into the doorway of Stevie's room, then sat down on the floor and leaned against the wall. "Listen, Mouse. Right this very minute, your dad is downstairs talking to mine."

"He is? He told me he was going for a walk."

"Well, he walked right over here, is what. I heard him tell Dad he's worried about us. Because of that book, and Betty trying to buy it."

"That's the most wonderful news I've heard in a long time," said Mouse.

"What?"

"That Dad is worried enough to talk to your dad. Do you know what I've been doing all afternoon?"

"Helping him in the store?"

"Thinking."

Lynn tried to understand. "You don't usually?"

"Just trying to figure things out."

"Why haven't you called me?"

"Because I didn't want any interruptions. I pulled down my shades, took off my shoes, and sat in the dark all afternoon, just letting thoughts come, and I really, truly think I've figured it out."

"Figured out *what*? Mouse, you're driving me nuts!"

"Why Mom left us."

"Why?"

"I think Mrs. Tuggle made her do it. I think it's all witchcraft."

"Mouse, how can you—?"

"Think about it, Lynn. It was during all that trouble with Mrs. Tuggle that Mom moved to Ohio."

"But . . . she didn't even *know* Mrs. Tuggle. Mrs. Tuggle didn't even know *her!*"

"They didn't have to know each other. According to *Spells and Potions*, a witch can put a spell on you without you ever having met her. I think it was all part of Mrs. Tuggle's plan to get Mom to leave Dad and move to Ohio, and your mother to move her study into Mrs. Tuggle's house, where she'd be under her spell. Then both of us would be motherless orphans, and this would drive us into Mrs. Tuggle's arms."

"But—"

"I feel *sure* of it, Lynn! I'm *glad* that Dad is over there talking about us. If he could just realize that

Mom didn't want to leave—that it was all Mrs. Tuggle's doing—maybe he could persuade her to come back."

Lynn didn't know what to say. She was convinced that her own mother had been under Mrs. Tuggle's spell, but to believe that all the trouble between the Beasleys had been caused by witchcraft—well, she just couldn't bear to see Mouse disappointed again.

"Go listen to what they're saying, Lynn!" Mouse said. "This could be the best thing that's happened yet!"

Lynn swallowed. "Okay. I'll talk to you later," she said, and hung up. For several minutes, however, she simply sat with her hand on the phone. No matter how weird things might seem around the neighborhood, she could not for one minute believe that Mrs. Tuggle had anything to do with the Beasley marriage breaking up. But she also knew how desperately Mouse wanted her mother back—enough to blame almost anyone, believe almost anything. Loneliness, Lynn decided, could be a dangerous thing.

She carried the phone back to its stand in the second-floor hallway. The murmur of men's voices still came from the living room below, and Lynn cautiously made her way down the first four steps of the stairs in her stocking feet until she was just close enough to make out their words.

". . . anything at all I can do to distract them. In

the meantime, I appreciate this very much." Mr. Beasley's voice.

"Anything either of us can think of to do, we'll keep in touch. The sooner we can work this out, the better. This has taken up far too much of the girls' time and energy as it is."

Lynn was dismayed to discover that the conversation was ending. She had thought they would sit there talking an hour or more. That's the way women would have done. Women seemed to go deeper into things, while men sort of scratched along the surface, careful not to make too big a dent, cause too much of a stir.

The sound of footsteps again, coming across the rug. Lynn crept back up to the landing and around the corner.

"I'm hoping that proposal for a new recreation center goes through," came her father's voice as the men reached the front door. "That would give the girls other activities to think about. We ought to get as many parents as we can to support it."

"Count me in. I'll certainly attend the hearing," said Mr. Beasley.

Lynn stayed in her room on the third floor for about twenty minutes before she ventured down again, and when she took her glass and saucer into the kitchen, found her father pouring himself some ginger ale, staring absently out into the dusk of the backyard.

"Thought I heard the doorbell a while ago," she said casually, putting her dishes in the sink.

"You did. Ed Beasley dropped in for a few minutes."

Lynn faked surprise. "What did he want?"

"Just a business matter," her father said.

How could her father say that? Lynn wondered. Wasn't it Dad who told her once that telling only half a truth is sometimes the same as telling a lie? But if she told him what she'd overheard, she'd have to admit she had been listening from the stairs. Which was worse? Eavesdropping or lying?

"Hey, kitten," said her dad. "Mom tell you what we're planning the last week of August? How does a week at the Indiana Dunes sound?"

"Sounds great!" Lynn said.

"Thought we might even stop somewhere along the way and do a little fishing. You wouldn't like to help me straighten out my tackle box tomorrow, would you?"

"Sure, I'll do it," Lynn said.

There were probably seventy things Lynn would have preferred doing on a Sunday besides cleaning out a tackle box, but Judith and Stevie helped, too, and it *was* sort of fun to sit on the back steps with the whole family, untangling hooks and lines, putting all the different sizes of brightly colored lures in separate compartments, and listening to Dad talk about which he used when.

The phone rang at three, and Lynn answered. It was Mouse.

"This is the first chance I've had to call you since Dad got home last night. He's kept me busy every minute. Help him make a pie, he said. Clean my room. Put my photos in an album. What happened last night? What did they say?"

"I hardly found out a thing," Lynn admitted ruefully. "When I went back to listen, your dad was getting ready to leave. I asked Dad later what they talked about, and he said it was just a business matter."

"Well, just knowing they were talking about us— about *it*—makes me feel better," Mouse told her.

"I've got to go," said Lynn. "After we finish straightening up Dad's tackle box, he's going to take us into town for milkshakes. They're trying to keep us occupied, Mouse, in case you haven't guessed."

"I guessed," Mouse said.

For a few days, the memory of Betty, Charlotte Ann, Kirsten, and the fifth-grade twins stalking into Mr. Beasley's bookstore was so chilling that Lynn and Mouse did not go near the creek. They stayed away from the school playground, even. The knowledge that their fathers were concerned made it all the more serious. But as one day followed another— the sky blue, the birds singing, the bees buzzing—the threat seemed less ominous somehow.

On Friday, as soon as Mother was settled at the

dining room table with her manuscript, Lynn asked Stevie, "What would you like to play this morning?"

Her little brother thought it over. "Um . . . go to the creek again and float things off the bridge?"

"Oh, I don't think that's such a good idea. Let's play here at home," Lynn suggested. She gathered together some raw potatoes, marshmallows, raisins, and toothpicks, and from these they made "people" out on the back porch.

Around ten, Mouse came around the corner of the house on her bike.

"Yum! Food!" she said as soon as she saw the marshmallow people.

Stevie held out one of his creations. "Here! Eat Mr. Fat-Belly!" he said, and Mouse obliged, nibbling at the marshmallow and raisins.

"I really feel great today, Lynn," she said, when Stevie went into the house for a drink of water. "Now that our dads are worried, we don't have to worry so much ourselves."

"Maybe," Lynn told her.

Stevie came back out, wiping his sleeve across his mouth. "Who wants to go for a bike ride?" he called out.

Lynn smiled. "You do, I'll bet. Okay, let's go. Come with us, Mouse."

Lynn got her bike and this time put Stevie on the handlebars, and headed down toward town.

They passed the library, McDonald's, the Sweet

Shoppe, Mr. Beasley's bookstore, the dollar store, and on to the statue at the end of the street, then circled around and came back, stopping to get a drink at the fountain in front of the bank.

"Did you see?" Mouse said as she leaned over the fountain.

"See what?"

"Who was standing around outside Dad's store? Kirsten and Betty. With her rat, of course."

"Maybe they're waiting for a bus or something."

"The bus stop's down the block, Lynn."

"Then maybe they're waiting to see if that woman comes in to buy *Spells and Potions.* So what? They'll have a long wait."

"But when they see that nobody comes for it, and Dad still won't sell it to them, they'll probably think of a way to steal it."

"If they did, your dad would have a pretty good idea who did, and would send the police after them."

"You're right," said Mouse. "Anyway, I feel so good today that *nothing* can make me worry!"

They rode the streets east of Main Street and west of Main Street, and finally, when it was almost noon, headed back up the steep hill to the Morleys'.

Lynn's mother had lunch on the table when they trooped into the kitchen.

"Will you stay and eat with us, Marjorie?" she asked. "We're having chicken salad, and sliced peaches with ice cream."

"Sure!" Mouse was in a chair before Lynn had even finished washing Stevie's hands at the sink.

"I've almost finished a first draft, and I really like it," Mother said as she put a box of crackers on the table. "Usually I don't start to like a manuscript— *really* like it—until the second draft, but some of the scenes came so easily for me, as though someone else was dictating the words and I was merely writing them down."

She sat on a chair across from Lynn and poured lemonade in all the glasses. "It's based on a true story about my grandmother and a plague of grasshoppers. But in *my* book, there are these two girls who—"

"Don't, Mother." The words were out of Lynn's mouth before she could stop them.

Mrs. Morley paused. "You don't want to know the story?"

"Why don't you wait till you finish all three drafts —until you've got it just the way you really want it— and then let us read it ourselves."

"Yeah, we'll be your critics, Mrs. Morley," Mouse volunteered. "We'll tell you if anything's wrong."

Mother laughed gaily. "Okay, you two, it's a deal."

Mouse and Mother chattered on, but Lynn was thinking about Mother's manuscript. The last book Mother had been working on—the one she had been writing at Mrs. Tuggle's, the manuscript that had burned up in the house along with the old woman herself—was a story that, in part, came true. Last

September, when Lynn and Mouse were walking home one day with Mother from Mrs. Tuggle's, she had told them the plot of that story. It was about a girl named Ann who suspected that her sister was a witch, just as Lynn had once suspected Judith. There was an old woman in the story, too, and at the end, when the old woman and Ann were alone together, their shadows mingling in the light of a candle, Ann discovered that it was not really her sister, after all, who was becoming a witch, but she herself, and when she looked in the mirror, she saw, instead, the face of the old woman.

Lynn shivered involuntarily, and realized that Mother had noticed.

"Lynn, are you *cold*? Surely you're not catching something, are you?"

Lynn managed a smile. "Just swallowed an ice cube," she said, and everyone laughed. Stevie even had to try it next. Lynn hated it when she had to fib. But she wondered why Mother hadn't remembered how closely her plot in the old manuscript resembled what had happened in real life. There had even been a fire somewhere in Mother's book. And then her remark just now about someone dictating the words . . . Did this mean that Mrs. Tuggle was still around —her influence, at least?

"I don't know why you don't write about mountain climbers or acrobats or something," Lynn said after a moment. "Why do you always have to write about people like Mouse and me and Judith and Stevie?"

"Because I don't *know* anyone else as well as you children."

That's what Lynn was afraid of. "Write a book about Dad, then."

Mother smiled. "Maybe someday I will."

What also bothered Lynn was that everyone else seemed to be feeling extra good today—Mouse because she was convinced her mother would come home once she discovered she'd been bewitched, and Mother because she had finished a first draft of her novel. Was Lynn the only one who realized how dangerously out of hand things were getting? Mouse had seen Betty and Kirsten hanging around outside her father's bookstore, but had that bothered her? Only for a minute.

Lynn considered calling Dr. Long that evening after Mouse had gone home, and tried to rehearse what she would say. *Some other girls are becoming witches; Mouse thinks her mother's bewitched. . . .* She couldn't get away with telling him just that. He'd want to know the details. The gulls with the broken necks, the fingers of fog, the purple-hooded flowers that hummed . . . Would any of it sound urgent? One of her worst fears was that she might go to him too soon, that he would not believe her, and would tell her parents she was imagining it all. On the other hand, what if she went to him too late?

Judith ran in about two to get her bathing suit to go to the pool with Ken Phillips, and Mother and Stevie went to the park. Lynn and Mouse, sitting on the back porch swing, playing Old Maid, waited until they saw the crows and gulls gathering over the meadow, and then they knew that the five girls were having their meeting. That was the sign.

"Shall we go?" Lynn said.

"I suppose." Mouse reluctantly put down her cards.

The sun, which had shone so brightly before, was covered now by clouds, but the air was dry, not damp. Except for a brief rain more than a week ago, there had been very little this summer, and the grass seemed to crackle and snap beneath their feet.

The worst part about spying on Betty and her crowd was having to take the long way around. Lynn and Mouse could have got there in five minutes if they had simply walked through the Morleys' garden and the back gate, across the field, and down the hill to the creek where the purple-hooded flowers grew. But the other girls would have seen them the moment they reached the crest of the hill.

Instead, once they left the back gate, they walked along the fence, following a winding, little-used path overgrown with weeds and prickly bushes that reached out and scratched them as they passed. On through the hickory grove they went, until they came out into the wild blueberry bushes on the other side. Then, going downhill a short distance, they crouched

unseen only thirty feet away from the place the five girls held their meetings. Since Betty lived on the far side of Cowden's Creek, she and her friends usually came from the other side. The girls had already gathered.

This time, both Lynn and Mouse froze in their tracks when they took in the scene below. Betty was standing at the water's edge with her arms outstretched, and on each of her arms there was a bird—a crow on one, a gull on the other. Charlotte Ann and the fifth-grade twins had made a circle around the candle. All of them were looking up at the trees, which seemed alive with crows. The birds preened and pranced, cawing and screeching, their beady eyes on Betty. And above the tree, the gulls circled, adding their shrieks to the din. Betty's head was tipped back, eyes closed.

"*Abigar*," she called.

"*Abigar*," the other girls chanted.

And, as if on command, another large white gull sailed down through the air, circled once, and lit on Betty's right shoulder.

Just as Mrs. Tuggle used to do. Worse yet, each girl wore one of the purple-hooded flowers in her hair, pinned under a barrette or tucked behind one ear.

"*Shaddar*," Betty commanded.

An agitated crow at the top of the tree walked nervously back and forth.

"*Shaddar*," the other girls responded in unison.

The huge bird spread his wings, then floated down to his mistress below and lit on Betty's other shoulder.

Suddenly Lynn felt a hand on her arm—a hand that wasn't Marjorie's—and she and Mouse whirled around to see Kirsten, her eyes huge and angry-looking, the skin blue above her white-blond eyebrows.

"Spies!" she yelled down to the others, and Lynn felt herself being pulled in the direction of Cowden's Creek.

chapter eight

She had never realized that Kirsten was so strong. It reminded her of the strength in Mrs. Tuggle's bony hands and legs, strange for such a frail-looking old woman. As Lynn tried to wrestle her wrist free, her captor seemed to loom large over her, like a Viking girl of long ago. How could she possibly hang on to both Lynn and Mouse without either of them managing to loosen her grip?

They half slid, half tumbled down the steep path to the bank below where the other girls waited—the fifth-grade twins looking gleeful at the catch, Charlotte Ann unsmiling, and Betty downright menacing. The birds screeched and flew back up to the sky.

"Let go!" Lynn demanded, struggling. "We have as much right to be here as you do. You don't own the creek."

"They were up in the blueberries," Kirsten said to the others.

Why hadn't she realized that Kirsten was missing from the circle? Lynn wondered. How could she and Mouse have expected to go day after day, spying and listening in, without one of the girls ever seeing them? It seemed ridiculous now.

"You saw," said Betty accusingly.

"N-no, we were j-just . . ." Mouse stammered.

"You heard," said Charlotte Ann.

Lynn hated the way Mouse caved in so readily. "We know what you're up to," she told the others. "Don't think we don't."

"*What* are we up to?" asked one of the twins.

And so Lynn said it, the "W" word: "Witchcraft."

The laughter of the five girls sounded like the cackle of crows, ringing out sharp and jagged over the softness of the meadow. It was when it cut off suddenly that Lynn became even more aware of the hum and, as she glanced about, it seemed that all the purple flowers had turned in her direction, watching from under their purple hoods, their faces hidden. *Witch's flowers. Witch's weeds.*

She plunged ahead before her courage could give out: "Whatever you try to do, we'll figure it out," she said. "If you cause any trouble, we'll stop you."

Why didn't Mouse help? Why did she just crouch there on the ground where she had landed when Kirsten shoved her, eyes huge, not saying anything at all?

"Come on, Mouse. Let's go," Lynn said.

But Betty blocked the path. "What's your hurry?" she said, a smile teasing her lips. "You just got here. You wanted to hang around with us, remember? You asked if you could join? Well, now we're letting you in. Now you can be members."

"Of what?" Lynn asked.

"The Coventry Club," said Charlotte Ann.

Lynn felt her legs actually shaking as they did once when she'd had the flu. She tried to keep her voice steady but noticed the slight tremor when she spoke: "Why do you want us now? You didn't then."

"Then was then and now is now," Betty told her. "We learned something, that's all—that we need more members. If you and Mouse join, we'll have seven."

"What do you need seven for?" Lynn asked, already guessing.

"Anything. Everything," Kirsten responded. "What does it matter? Do you want to join or not?"

"What kind of a club is it?" Lynn asked, wanting to get as much information as possible before she said no. "What do you do?"

"We can't tell you that until you join. It's secret," said one of the fifth-grade twins.

"But we stand up for each other." It was Betty talking now. "We'll go after anyone who's against you."

Lynn looked straight into her eyes: "It's a witches' coven, right?"

Again the laughter of the five girls seemed harsh and sharp in the air. They formed a circle around her as they laughed, and the crows and gulls joined in. *"Caw-ha-ha! Caw-ha-ha!"* The sound seemed to echo along the creek.

Lynn looked over at Mouse. She seemed dazed, her eyes huge behind her glasses, her full attention on Betty, lips slightly apart, hands resting on her knees. And now Betty focused entirely on Mouse. Kneeling down next to her, her face even with Marjorie's, she looked into her eyes as she talked:

"When you join the Coventry Club," she said, "you learn how to protect yourself so bad things can't happen. To you or your family. If we have enough power, we not only stop things from happening to us but we can make things happen to other people instead."

"If you *don't* join, well, we can't promise *what* will happen," warned Charlotte Ann.

"Your mother's way off in Ohio, isn't she?" Kirsten put in. "Think about her. You can even learn things that will help keep *her* safe. But if you *don't* join, things could happen."

"T-to my mother?" Mouse whispered.

"Don't *listen* to them, Mouse!" Lynn cried. "They're trying to scare you. They can't hurt your mother! Don't—"

"Stop her!" Betty said.

In an instant, Lynn was on her back, Kirsten holding her arms down, the fifth-grade twins holding her legs.

"Mouse!" she screamed. "Run! Get your dad! Tell him—"

A hand clamped over her mouth and the crows, watching overhead, shrieked and flapped their wings.

And then, as Lynn thrashed about on the ground, she saw Charlotte Ann leaning over her, holding a purple-hooded flower that she thrust into Lynn's face.

A faint hum came from this single flower. The petals seemed to fill Lynn's nostrils, and for a moment she felt she could not breathe. The air above her face clouded over, like mist, and in the fog, shapes came and went—faces, fingers. . . . She tried to call out to Mouse again, but the hum was growing louder and louder, or perhaps her voice was getting fainter and fainter, until she could no longer hear herself. She seemed to be sinking farther and farther down a deep dark well . . . deeper . . . farther . . . deeper and farther. . . .

She was conscious at last of being cold. It seeped through her clothes and into her back, her legs, the marrow of her bones. Lynn was not even sure where she was. She had dreamed she was down in a hole, but felt a breeze now on her skin.

It was a struggle to open her eyes, as though she had been sleeping for days, and her eyelids had glued themselves shut. But when she managed to open them at last and look about her, she saw the same gray sky, same clouds, same tree branches overhead —even a gull or two. The girls, however, were gone.

Lynn could not imagine that she had simply fallen asleep. Had they fought? Had she been knocked unconscious? She raised one hand to her face and felt around for bumps and bruises—blood, even. Nothing.

"Mouse?" she said weakly.

There was no answer.

Lynn stiffly hoisted herself up on one hand and looked around. Mouse was gone.

"Mouse!" Lynn struggled to her feet and looked about her. There was no sign of a struggle, no trail in the weeds of someone having been dragged away.

"Mouse!" She was screaming now. A crow lit on a tree limb above and strutted about, mocking her. *"Caw!"* it cackled. *"Caw! Caw!"* Some gulls circling about in the sky just beyond chipped in with their taunting *"Eeeek! Eeeek!"*

Lynn ran, stumbling, half falling and catching herself, and barreled on—up the shorter path to the crest of the hill, then across the field to the Morleys' back gate. She burst through it and into the garden, then on across the yard.

Mother was on the back porch shelling peas, Stevie helping.

"Mom! Did Mouse come up here?"

"No. I thought she was with you."

Lynn ran around the side of the house. Marjorie's bike was still there. She grabbed her own, and wondered if she could trust herself to ride. Felt as though her head were twice as big as usual, twice as heavy, as though it were tipping uncontrollably to one side or the other. She pedaled as far as the street, then let her feet rest as the bike picked up speed and went careening, bumpily, down the brick pavement.

Rounding the corner at the bottom, she went two blocks over to a side street until she came to the third house on the right. She leapt off her bike and let it fall on the grass in the front yard, ran up on the porch and banged on the door.

No answer.

"Mouse?" she called, and waited some more. No footsteps—no sounds at all from inside. She checked the back door. Locked. Swallowing, her heart pounding, she got on her bike again and rode over to the school, across the playground to the benches where Betty and Charlotte Ann and the others sometimes sat. But the benches were empty. Overhead, however, several crows and a gull seemed to be following. Watching. Waiting.

Lynn didn't care. She had to keep looking. Had to find Mouse. She rode back out to the street and down into the business district, stopping, her sides aching, outside Mr. Beasley's bookstore. But she could see almost the whole shop through the wide display window, and Mr. Beasley was working alone. Lynn did not want to have to tell him all that had happened if she could help it. *Why did you go down there?* he would ask. *Why did you get involved?* If she could only find Mouse . . .

She rode to the statue at the end of the street and stopped to rest. The birds circled the statue, and finally a crow came down and lit on its shoulder. The other birds flew even higher, then headed off in a new direction.

The cemetery! It was the last place she could think of to look. If Mouse wasn't there, then Lynn would have to tell Mr. Beasley. She shoved off and rode to a side street, crossing the bridge in town where Cowden's Creek flowed through the business district, then taking a narrow blacktopped road on the other side that turned toward the graveyard.

It was as though the birds led the way, flying in wide circles, looking back every so often to see whether or not Lynn was coming. What if Betty and her gang were there? What if they were holding Mouse prisoner until she joined their coven? Perhaps she should go back to town and get Marjorie's father before she went any farther, but her feet pedaled on, and when she came to the iron gate, nudged it open with the front wheel of her bike, and rode up through the tumbledown tombstones until she came to the place where she and Mouse used to meet when they wanted to talk in secret.

And there she was. Mouse sat between two marble angels who were holding a marble book. She was alone, leaning back against the angels, legs stuck out stiffly before her, each hand clutching one of the cold stone hands of an angel. She did not move.

Lynn stopped and slipped quietly off her bike, not

wanting to startle Mouse, then finally tiptoed around into her line of vision.

"Mouse?" she said softly.

Marjorie turned her head, looked at her, but said nothing.

Lynn walked over slowly and crouched down beside the tombstone. "Mouse?" she said again. "Are you okay?"

"Why shouldn't I be?"

"What happened back there? I opened my eyes and everybody was gone. *You* were gone! Why did you leave me? I was afraid they'd kidnapped you, and I've been looking *every*where!"

"You didn't want to come, so we just left you."

"*We?*" Lynn stared. It was Mouse's voice, all right, and the girl on the tombstone *looked* like Mouse, but it wasn't the friend Lynn had always known. "What do you mean *we?* Have you joined them? *Mouse!* You didn't!"

"It's only a club. The Coventry Club."

"It's a coven! A witches' coven! Mouse, you *know* that!"

Mouse still didn't move. Sat looking down at her feet. "Maybe they can help me get Mom back."

"What are you saying?" Lynn lunged forward and grabbed her by the sleeves. "Did you join? You *did*, didn't you?" She shook her hard, and something tumbled from Mouse's hair down onto her shoulder, then

into her lap. It was a purple-hooded flower. *The Witch Weed.*

Lynn stared in horror. Then suddenly she grabbed the flower, leapt onto her bike, and took off.

She rode blindly, the flower in her hand. She wanted to stamp on it, ride over it, mash it, burn it. Should she go tell Mr. Beasley what was happening? Tell her own father? When she reached the business district again, she had still another thought. She looked at the clock on the courthouse. Four forty-five. She would chance it.

She went directly to the school and came to a screeching stop at the bike rack. Even during the regular school year, few teachers stayed past four o'clock. And here it was summer. Lynn realized that Dr. Long might have gone home hours ago. But as she started toward the building, she saw him just getting into his car at the far end of the parking lot.

"Dr. Long!" Her mouth felt dry, her lips chapped, as she leapt off her bike and ran over.

"Lynn?"

"Help me!"

He looked at her curiously. "What's wrong?"

"Please. I need to talk."

"All right. A little or a lot?"

"A lot."

"Then let's go inside to my office."

*

Even before she sat down, Lynn laid the purple-hooded flower on his desk. "Here," she said.

"For me?"

She shook her head. "It's not what you think. It's terrible. Terrible things are happening!"

"Want to fill me in?"

Lynn closed her eyes and sighed shakily. "It all sounds so weird. You'll think I'm nutty."

"Forget nutty. Just say what you like."

His voice was so quiet and reassuring that Lynn's eyes filled with tears and she hated that. Dopey Lynn. She bit her lip and waited a moment until the tears subsided. Only one of them managed to trickle out the corner of her eye, and she wiped it hastily.

"I very much wanted this to be a normal summer," she said. "And then, there was this smell, and I heard the humming."

"Someone humming?"

"No. Like a low buzz, sort of. Mouse and I walked down to Cowden's Creek—where we threw the eye, remember?—and there were these strange purple flowers all along the bank. They seemed to have just sprung up overnight, and . . . now, I know this sounds weird . . . the humming seems to come from them. And there's this smell—like gas, almost. When we're down there, the flowers even turn together, like they're watching, listening. I suppose it could just be the wind. . . ."

"That's certainly the likeliest explanation, don't you think?"

"Anyway, we decided to ignore them. The flowers. The humming. And then one day we rode our bikes over to the school to see what the other girls were doing this summer—make new friends, like you said —and there were these five girls that Mouse and I always *thought* were nice, but . . . They wouldn't let us join their club. So we decided, okay, we'd find someone else, and then . . ."

Lynn paused wearily, trying to sort things through in her head, figure out what exactly had happened when. "One night we found a dead seagull on our porch at the same time Mr. Beasley found one on his. And we discovered that these five girls have been meeting down at the creek, among the flowers. And they've been chanting some of the same words that Mrs. Tuggle used to chant, and crows fly down and land on their arms, just the way they did for her. Crows and gulls."

Dr. Long studied her intently, saying nothing.

"It's not just a club, it's witchcraft. I'm sure of it," Lynn continued breathlessly. "And somehow they found out about the rare book in Mr. Beasley's book-store, *Spells and Potions*—the only book Mouse and I have to protect us from witchcraft—and they've been trying to buy it. But the worst thing happened this afternoon. Mouse and I have been spying on the girls when they went down to the creek, and they caught us. They dragged us down into the middle of their circle, and this time they said we could join."

"So they've had a change of heart."

"Dr. Long! They said we could join because they need two more people. That's just what Mouse and I learned from reading *Spells and Potions*. A witch's coven needs seven people."

"Lynn, *playing* at being witches isn't the same as really being a witch, you know. If there are such things."

"I'm frightened. You've got to believe me. They call their club the *Coven*try Club. And they talked about how they could keep horrible things from happening to Mouse's mother if Mouse would just join. I was begging her not to, and they wrestled me to the ground and pushed one of these weeds in my face. I blacked out. When I came to, everyone was gone. I found Mouse sitting in the cemetery by herself, with this witch flower in her hair. She's joined. She wants to protect her mother. So I brought it to you."

"Lynn, this is sounding pretty fantastic, you know."

"Yes, I know."

He reached out and picked up the flower. "What do you want me to do with this?"

"Find out what it is."

"Well, it's certainly nothing I've seen around here before, I'll grant you, but I'm no authority on plants. Are you sure that there wasn't a fight—that you weren't stunned for a moment or something?"

"Positive. We didn't fight. The last thing I remember was this flower in my face, and the smell of a sort of perfumy gas."

"I tell you what. I'm leaving town this evening for a few days to attend a psychology conference in Bloomington, and I can take the flower to the horticulture department at the university there. Maybe they can identify it for us. But I don't think that's going to solve your problem with these girls, Lynn."

She wanted to cry, but didn't. Disappointment tugged at the corners of her mouth. "You think this is all just girls fighting over a club. Right?"

"I'll admit it sounds that way to me."

"Well, these girls are talking about making things happen to other people, not just *keeping* things from happening. And the whole business has got my dad worried. Mouse's father, too. *Please* believe me."

The psychologist thought for a long time before he answered. "I believe you're telling me what you think happened, just as I asked you to. And I certainly agree that all of this is worth looking into. I definitely want to see you again. We'll have to leave things there until I get back. Okay?"

"Okay." Lynn got up. "You promised to keep an open mind, remember?"

"Wide as a bathtub," the psychologist said, and opened the door for her.

Lynn decided she couldn't stop just yet. She rode back to Mr. Beasley's bookstore, determined to tell him everything that had happened that afternoon, so he could keep an eye on Mouse.

There were two women at the counter when Lynn came in, so she had to wait while Mr. Beasley wrapped their purchases and gave them their change. Suddenly her eye fell on the display case behind the counter and then her heart almost stopped beating. *Spells and Potions* was gone. The space where the book had been was empty. Had Betty or Charlotte Ann managed to steal it? Or was it possible that while she had blacked out that afternoon, Mouse had got hold of the book and given it to the others?

"Mr. Beasley!" she said as the two women went out the door. "The book! *Spells and Potions!* It's gone!"

"Hello, Lynn," Marjorie's father said cheerfully. "Yes, I know it's gone. I sold it."

"S-sold it?"

"Yes. Found a buyer. Not those girls either. A gentleman made me an offer and I accepted."

Lynn stared in disbelief. *Betty's father, who else?* He would give the book to Betty, and from then on, Lynn wouldn't stand a chance. Things were whirling completely out of control.

She didn't feel she could take any more. She didn't trust herself to say anything else without bawling, so she dashed outside and rode home. It was time to talk to her dad. Tell him everything. He was worried about her now, so maybe he'd listen. He had to. She'd wait until after dinner, when the family had scattered, then get him alone.

As she leaned her bike against the steps, she noticed that Marjorie's was gone. Mouse had come while she was out—come and gone like a shadow. She went inside, then realized that the worst hadn't happened yet; the worst was yet to come. Because there on the table, in a vase in the center, was a large bouquet of purple-hooded flowers, which all turned slightly as Lynn entered the kitchen, then bent their hooded heads again and remained still.

chapter nine

"Where did the flowers come from?" Lynn stood unmoving in the doorway.

Mother didn't even look up. "Aren't they unusual? Stevie and I just got back from a walk along the creek, and the whole bank is covered with them. Some kind of weed, I imagine, but I never noticed them down there before. Look. The purple just matches the violets in my wallpaper."

"They're like little people," said Stevie, coming into the kitchen from the porch. "See, Lynn?" He turned up one of the flowers to show her inside its hood, but all she could see was darkness. "Like little people wearing hats or something."

"Hoods," said Mother.

Lynn looked around. "Where's Dad?"

"He's changing his clothes. Call up and tell him dinner's ready, will you?"

Lynn went up to the bedrooms on the second floor, but realized that this was no time to try and talk to her father about all that had happened.

"Dinner's ready," she said, leaning against the wall outside his door.

"Be down in a second," he called. "How'd *your* day go, Lynn? Anything exciting happen?"

"Yeah. I was carried off by a group of thugs and knocked out cold and then these huge birds woke me up and I went searching for Mouse and found out she'd joined a secret society."

Her father chuckled. "Sure you want to be a psychiatrist and not a writer?" he said, coming out of the bedroom as he buttoned his sport shirt.

"And if I told you it was all true?"

"Then, sweetheart, I'd say you've been reading too much science fiction. What are we having for dinner?"

"Meat loaf." They started downstairs.

Judith was on the front porch saying good-bye to Ken Phillips. They'd probably see each other that evening, Lynn thought, and again the next day, but the way they looked into each other's eyes, you'd never know it.

Father gave them a passing glance as he turned at the bottom of the stairs and headed for the kitchen. "Ah, romance!" he said. "Maybe you could write romance novels, Lynn. There's certainly enough material around here lately to fill a few books."

When the family was gathered at last at the table, Judith sneezed. Then again.

"I think it's the flowers," she said. "What kind are they?"

"I don't know. Weeds, probably," said Mother. "Stevie and I found them by the creek."

"They're the weirdest things I ever saw," said Judith. "And they've got a really peculiar scent." She bent forward, inhaled, then sneezed again. "I'd swear I've smelled this scent before, but I can't remember where."

"Try," said Lynn.

"If I think of it, I'll tell you," Judith promised, and reached for the rolls.

At first it seemed like a normal dinner. It was a normal menu: meat loaf, baked potatoes, spinach salad, applesauce, and lemon pie for dessert. Lemon pie usually put Lynn's father and Judith in a good mood because they liked it best. Mother never ate more than a sliver, Stevie just ate the meringue, and Lynn ate only the crust.

But tonight, for some reason, when they got to dessert, there was tension in the air that wasn't usually there at mealtime.

"Stevie, for heaven's sake, if you only want the meringue, then don't take a whole piece," Mother snapped irritably. "I didn't make a pie just so you could maul it."

"I'll eat the crust on his piece," Lynn said hastily.

"That still leaves the filling looking like a dog's breakfast."

"Don't worry about it, Sylvia. I'll eat my piece and that, too," Father said.

It seemed for a few minutes that things would be okay again, and then Judith said, "I'm going over to Kenny's this evening to listen to a new CD."

"Judith, you're gone more than you're home," Father snapped. "The way you and Kenny were kissing on the porch, I thought he was sailing off to war or something."

Lynn glanced quickly at her father. What got into *him*? One minute he was trying to keep the peace and the next he was starting trouble. It just didn't sound like Father at all.

Judith blushed fiercely. "You were *watching*!"

"I just happened to look out the window," said Mr. Morley, "and I'm not sure I like the way you and Kenny carry on. But if you *are* going out tonight, make sure you've finished all your work around the house. This place has looked like a rat's nest lately."

"Richard!" said Mother hotly.

"I scrubbed the bathrooms already," Judith told him.

"Well, whoever's responsible for dusting the furniture isn't doing a very good job of it," Father continued. "There's been dust on my nightstand for over a week."

"I'm dusting tomorrow, Dad," Lynn told him. "I'll make sure I do a good job on your room."

Things quieted down for a time. *Now* maybe the arguing was over. Lynn waited until Stevie had eaten the meringue off his pie, then took his saucer and ate the crust from under the filling.

Judith, however, glared at her in disgust. "This family eats like *pigs*! Look at the mess they've made of that pie. If I ever invited Kenny here for dinner and they ate like that, I'd be embarrassed to death."

"We already *talked* about that," Lynn said. "Dad's going to eat it."

"Just the same, I—"

"I can*not* stand this bickering!" Mother yelled, holding her head. "Stop it! Stop it! Stop it!"

Lynn got out of her chair. "May I be excused?"

"Excused," said her father.

She went upstairs and sat down on her bed. So much for trying to talk to her father about witchcraft, she decided. Trying to talk to him about *any*thing. Was she being supersensitive? She didn't think so. Everyone had *seemed* to come to the table in a good mood. Then Judith had sneezed, and . . .

Lynn reached in the drawer by her bed and took out her journal. She was keeping a written account of all that had happened since the trouble had begun with Mrs. Tuggle. It had been weeks since she'd made an entry, and there was a lot to add. She had been writing for about fifteen minutes when Judith came in and walked on over to her side of the large bedroom.

"That was a pretty unpleasant meal," Judith said aloud as she flipped through the hangers in her closet. "I'm sorry I sounded off, Lynn. I think it's my allergy. I always seem to get nasty when my nose acts up." She took out a fresh shirt, held it against her in front of the mirror, then changed.

Lynn's pencil paused over her paper. "It wasn't just you," she said. "Dad and Mom were in a bad mood, too. I can't understand it. We were feeling so good before dinner."

"Maybe we're *all* allergic," Judith said, taking a brush and running it hard through her long dark hair, making it shine. She stopped brushing a minute and turned to Lynn. "I just remembered where I've smelled that scent—what it reminds me of, anyway: Mrs. Tuggle."

The pencil fell out of Lynn's hand. She stared.

"Don't you remember?" Judith said. "I don't think she wore perfume, exactly. But sometimes she had a strong, sort of sweetish scent—I always thought it was skin cream or something." She glanced at her watch. "Kenny's waiting. See you!" And she hurried out the door and on downstairs.

Judith, without realizing it, Lynn wrote, picking up her pencil again, *said exactly what I'm thinking: The flowers are responsible for what went on here tonight, and Mrs. T. is behind it all. I'm convinced now that the eye didn't get swept away by the current, or—if it did—that it left spores of evil behind—along the bank. And now, the hooded flowers . . .*

It took her a long time to get to sleep that night,

partly because she was listening for the phone, hoping Mouse would call, and partly because she knew Mouse wouldn't. How could she go the rest of the summer without the closest friend she'd had since first grade? All the things they'd done over the years, the places they'd gone, the secrets they'd shared . . . those long afternoons of talk . . .

Lynn rolled over on her stomach and allowed herself to cry. It wasn't just not having Mouse as a friend that upset her; it was her worry about what was happening to Mouse now. If Lynn only had *Spells and Potions* she might find something that would work to bring Mouse back, but the book was gone.

There were just too many things to worry about. Lynn gave up finally and fell asleep about two, long after Judith had come home and gone to bed, but it was an uneasy sleep. She dreamed she was standing in the parking lot at school waiting for Dr. Long to get back from his trip. His car pulled up and Lynn followed him inside, but when he opened his briefcase to take out the purple-hooded flower she had given him, Lynn had seen, tucked in one corner among his papers, the book *Spells and Potions.* She woke perspiring, her heart pounding. Dr. Long? Was it possible? What if *he* was in on this too? What if he told Betty and Charlotte Ann everything she told him?

Lynn got up and went down to the second-floor bathroom to splash cold water on her face. If she started being suspicious of everyone, she *would* be mentally ill. She had no reason to suspect the psychologist, but what if . . . ?

What if, her father used to say, *includes everything that could possibly happen.* And he was right. From now on she would distrust only those people she had any reason to suspect.

Lynn knew she couldn't sleep anymore so she went on downstairs and poured herself some orange juice, trying not to look at the purple flowers. She took her glass out on the back-porch glider to watch the sunrise over the meadow.

Her heart ached with missing Mouse, though. Every day, for almost as long as she could remember, she woke up thinking about what they were going to do together. Now Mouse had another group of girls to go around with, but she wasn't happy. Lynn had known that just by looking at her—the forlorn way she had been sitting alone in the cemetery. Somehow Lynn had to help.

Okay, she told herself. *Make a plan. First tell Father everything. Second, tell Mr. Beasley everything. Third . . .*

There was a faint noise from somewhere inside, and Lynn wondered what it was. A familiar sound, but she couldn't quite place it. She was sure that no one in the family was up yet. It wasn't even five o'clock, and the first streaks of pink and gray were just now showing on the horizon.

Lynn inched cautiously back into the kitchen, looking around, half expecting to see the purple flowers move about on the table. They were not moving, but they were giving off a definite hum.

"Shut up," Lynn told them.

This, however, was not the noise she had heard. It was more like a drawer sliding shut, or a door closing, or . . . The screen door, that was it! Like someone had softly opened and closed the screen.

Lynn padded out into the hallway in her bare feet. And there, sticking out from under the front door, was one corner of a folded notepaper.

Lynn rushed to the window in the music room and looked out, waiting for her eyes to grow accustomed to the dark of the street. No one was there. She went back into the hallway and picked up the notepaper, then sat down on the bottom stair and read it by the light of the small table lamp:

Lynn, it said on the outside, in Mouse's handwriting, and on the inside: *You don't need to come to work in Dad's store anymore. We'll ask someone else.*

That much Lynn might have expected. It hurt, but didn't surprise her. What took her breath away, however—what made her stomach sick, almost—was the signature. It did not say "Mouse" or even "Marjorie." *Sevena*, the note was signed, the name Mrs. Tuggle had given her.

Lynn could stand it no longer. She took a flashlight and went out the back door and around to the tool shed. She found a spray bottle of weed killer, and then, like a murderer with a knife, crept back inside and started toward the kitchen table.

The hum grew louder and higher, and the flowers moved, as though backing away from her.

Lynn took another step. The hum became words: "Suck the honey from my lips. . . ."

Lynn lifted the spray bottle.

"Dance upon my fingertips. . . ."

She placed her finger on the nozzle.

"When the darkness tolls the hour, I shall have you in my . . ."

Lynn pressed the nozzle. A spray of poison shot out of the bottle. Lynn walked slowly around the table, directing the poison at the large bouquet. Almost immediately, as though they were insects, the flowers fell over, pale and withered, and the singing stopped.

Good, Lynn said to herself. And then, aloud: "Good, good, good!"

Encouraged, she tiptoed back upstairs, past her parents' room, and on up to the large bedroom on the third floor. She changed from her pajamas to shorts, T-shirt, and sneakers, and went down again. There was a large metal can of weed killer in the tool shed, so Lynn took both that and the spray bottle and headed out across the backyard. She crossed the garden, opened the back gate, and started over the field toward the creek below.

The sky was still gray, and the meadow enveloped

in mist, but Lynn could see well enough to follow the path. Ahead, the mist seemed to form itself into shapes once again—a nose, a chin, a neck, a shoulder bony as a doorknob. Dark holes appeared in the fog where Mrs. Tuggle's eyes would be—hollow as the eye sockets in a skull. The cloud of a face rushed her as Lynn approached until it enveloped her entirely, but still she plodded on, feeling her way.

On the creek bank, the purple-hooded flowers seemed asleep, heads tucked down, leaves heavy with dew. Lynn walked as far in one direction as she could find any flowers at all, and then carefully bent down, aiming the nozzle directly up into the opening of the first purple flower. She pressed her finger.

There was a scream, and Lynn leapt to one side, staring. Then she realized that the scream came from a crow overhead that was watching. Determinedly, she moved to the next flower and the next. Looking over her shoulder, she saw the first flowers begin to droop.

"Good!" she said gleefully.

There must have been hundreds, she wasn't sure. Lynn soon ran out of weed killer in the bottle and filled it again from the can. By the time she was half done, her back ached painfully.

The sky was full light. More and more birds were gathering overhead, all flying in circles directly above her, but Lynn tried not to notice. The weed killer was running low, and when she had used the very last, there were still twenty or more flowers left.

She wearily rubbed her arms and tried to think. She could always wait until the stores opened, then take all her money and go buy some more. But it seemed important somehow to do it now—to kill all the flowers at once. She wondered what else she might use from either the medicine cabinet or the kitchen that might work.

Salt.

Lynn remembered reading somewhere, in *Spells and Potions*, that if you put salt under a witch's chair, it prevented her from rising. Maybe it would have some effect on the flowers. She ran quickly home and searched through the cupboard for the large round blue and white box of salt, taking both that and the metal shaker Mother kept on the stove top.

This time, the crows and gulls were waiting. When she reached the crest of the hill, the sudden screeching and cawing almost deafened her. As she started down, their circle in the sky above became a V, and they came at her like dive bombers, swooping low, then sailing off again. Lynn covered her head, waiting until they flew away, but when she moved on, they came again, this time letting their wings graze her head.

When she reached the bank and the birds swooped again, she used the saltshaker as her weapon, flinging the salt toward each bird as it dived. This time the gulls flew off, and the crows retreated to a tree on the bank where they hopped about in agitation, cawing and scolding.

Lynn set to work, sprinkling each plant with salt and filling the shaker again and again, carefully gauging the amount so as to have enough to go around. She dared not wait to see what happened, because the sun was up and soon her parents would be having breakfast. Taking the empty weed killer containers back home, she put them in the tool shed, placed the empty saltshaker back on the stove, and was just pouring herself some cereal when Mother came into the kitchen.

"Did you hear all that ruckus a while ago?" Mother asked. "Sounded like a menagerie out there in the field."

"Yeah," Lynn said. "But I was awake already."

Mrs. Morley took a few more steps toward the coffee maker, then stopped. "Oh, my goodness!" she said.

Lynn turned. Mother was staring at the flowers on the table. Would she ask? Would she guess?

"Well, these certainly didn't last long," Mother said. "I guess that's the difference between weeds and flowers. If they'd lasted, every florist in town would be out there picking some."

"I guess so," said Lynn. "Want me to throw them out?"

"Might as well."

With great satisfaction, Lynn picked up the limp stems and carried them outside. Crunching them in her hands, squeezing them until purple juice ran down her wrists, she wrung them as she would wring out a washcloth, then dropped them in the trash. When she got inside she scrubbed and scrubbed, wanting every last trace of them gone.

And sure enough, when the family came down to breakfast, everyone was in a good mood again. *Coincidence*, her father would say. But no one noticed that the flowers were gone, no one seemed to remember the quarreling that had gone on at supper, and Mother, luckily, decided to make pancakes for breakfast instead of scrambled eggs so she didn't discover there was no salt in the shaker. Lynn knew she would have to refill it by dinnertime.

"What a glorious Saturday!" Father said, drinking the last of his coffee. "How shall I spend it? Reading out under a tree? Working in the yard? Going to the pool? Playing golf?"

"I haven't played golf in years," said Mother. "I wonder if I still can."

"That's settled, then. We'll find out; golf it is," Father told her.

"Somebody will have to watch Stevie. . . ."

"I will," Judith volunteered. "Lynn's got to work at the bookstore."

"Not today. Mr. Beasley doesn't need me this week," Lynn said.

"Well, I'll still do it. You've had him on weekdays, so it's my turn," Judith told her.

It all sounded so ordinary, so natural, Lynn thought. *Mr. Beasley doesn't need me this week.* Nobody knew that her heart was breaking. In a few days, though, Mother would notice that Mouse hadn't been over at all, and would begin asking questions. How could Lynn possibly answer without telling her everything?

As soon as the breakfast dishes were done, Lynn set out for the creek again to examine the flowers. The ones she had sprayed with weed killer had flopped over on their sides, but the ones she had sprinkled with salt looked very peculiar—larger and thicker, coarse and ugly, even more menacing than they had before. She couldn't understand it! Salt shouldn't have made them grow! But *Spells and Potions* had said nothing about using salt to *kill* witches. Maybe all it did was limit their power.

She had to buy more weed killer to be sure. Lynn went back home to count the money in her drawer. In spite of the money she had earned from the bookstore, she had bought a pair of Nikes recently, and had only three dollars and forty-six cents. That wasn't enough. The price tag on the spray bottle had said $7.99. Maybe Mouse had some. Maybe . . . And then she remembered that Mouse would not help her. *Could* not.

Perhaps, Lynn thought, if she did all her weekly

chores and did them extra well, she could get her allowance one day early and even an advance on next week's.

She made her bed, changed the sheets on Stevie's, dusted all the furniture throughout the house, and ran the vacuum over the downstairs carpet. Then she took the dust mop to the bedroom floors. This meant picking up Stevie's things, but she did so without complaining. It meant picking up Judith's shoes and socks and hair rollers, but Lynn did that too. The kitchen and bathrooms were Judith's responsibility, but the rest of the house would be spotless when her parents came back from the golf course.

Up in the master bedroom, Lynn poked the dust mop in all the corners, careful to get the closet floor as well as the baseboards. She not only poked under the bed, but got down on her hands and knees to make sure there wasn't a dust ball left that her father could complain about.

Thunk. The dust mop hit something halfway under. Lynn put her head down until it touched the floor. There was a paper sack far under the bed. She paused, wondering, then pushed it with the dust mop until she could reach it from the other side. She walked around to see what it was.

For a moment or two, she sat with the sack on her knees. She knew without even thinking about it that she should not open it. Knew that whatever was inside was her parents' business, not hers.

Against her better judgment, however, her fingers fumbled with the fold at the top of the sack. She would take one quick peek, and if it was something she shouldn't see, she'd close it right back up again.

Looking around to make sure no one was watching, Lynn unfolded the top, opened the sack and looked inside. Her heart leapt. There at the bottom was *Spells and Potions.*

chapter ten

She could not understand. For a moment, Lynn could not even feel. She seemed to have lost all sensation in her hands as she held the book.

Her *father*? *He* was the "gentleman" who had made an offer to Mr. Beasley? *He* had paid $2,000 for *Spells and Potions*? She stared incredulously.

There was one moment of doubt for which Lynn was ashamed afterward—one brief, heart-stopping minute when she wondered if the father she had always loved was himself caught up in Mrs. Tuggle's scheme. But then she knew, as surely as she knew the fingers on her hand, that he loved her. Why he had this book, she wasn't sure. Whether he was studying it, she didn't know. What she did know, however, was that just as her father loved her and would do anything he could to protect her, she in turn loved Mouse and had to do what she could to save her.

She could hear Judith's and Stevie's voices from outside as they played in Stevie's sandbox by the side of the house.

"Look, the tunnel's almost done," Judith was saying. "Watch, and you'll see my hand come out the other side."

Stevie gave a delighted squeal. "Let's build another tunnel over here," he said.

They'd be out there for a while. Lynn's heart beat faster. This was her chance to read all she could. She put the sack back under her parent's bed, took the dust mop outside to shake it, then carried *Spells and Potions* up to her room. Her parents probably wouldn't be back until late afternoon, and Stevie was Judith's for the day.

Her hands actually trembled as she carefully placed the rare book with its fragile pages on her bed. She had to work quickly and use every minute well. There was no time to read pages and pages of material that didn't help right now. What she was looking for was something she could give Mouse to protect her from evil. Gently she thumbed through the pages, reading the section headings: SABBAT, FA-MILIAR, NIGHTSHADE AND OTHER POISONS, DEMONS, EVIL, WARLOCKS, ANIMISM, CHARMS, POTIONS, SOR-CERY, TIDES . . .

She had decided to read the section on CHARMS when she heard Judith and Stevie coming upstairs. She slipped the book under her pillow, got out her photo album, and worked at adding some pictures that had been accumulating in her drawer.

"It's warm, but it's still glorious outside, Lynn," Judith said.

Stevie held up his arms to show the sand still stuck on them. "We're making a city in the sandbox," he announced. "Judith's going to build a racetrack for my cars."

"Well, maybe I'll go out after a while," Lynn said. "I'm just organizing stuff in my room."

"I've made sandwiches," Judith told her. "Yours is in the fridge when you want it. I'm going to take Stevie to the park and we'll eat ours there."

"A picnic!" said Stevie happily as they went back down again.

Lynn couldn't believe her good luck. She would have the whole house and *Spells and Potions* as well all to herself. For several hours she read and made notes. There were whole pages of mystic symbols that could be chalked on doorposts to protect against witchcraft. Red pepper and sulphur sprinkled throughout a house offered defense against spells. Ashes, the book said, could be used as protection against witches, and should a witch burn to death, it was necessary that her ashes be scattered to the winds to be sure that her power was extinguished. . . .

Lynn put the book down and stared at the wall. Maybe that was the whole problem: Mrs. Tuggle's ashes had not been scattered after her death. Lynn was not even sure they had been found—just bulldozed under.

She heard Judith and Stevie coming back from the

park, so she put *Spells and Potions* in the paper sack under her parents' bed exactly as she'd found it. She was on her way downstairs to eat her sandwich when Judith and Stevie came in. Little Stevie sprawled on the glider on the back porch, one foot on the floor, rocking back and forth, and in a matter of minutes was sound asleep.

"I mean it, Lynn, it's too nice a day to stay inside," Judith said as she went into the hall to call Ken Phillips.

Lynn sat staring down at her plate, rolling crumbs from her sandwich between her finger and thumb. She had found nothing in *Spells and Potions* so far about how to break a spell once it had entrapped someone—namely, Mouse. And Lynn did not know for sure whether Mouse was truly under a spell or had joined the witches' coven out of fear, or whether it was her hope that somehow they could, all of them together, work their power to bring her mother home again. Even if Lynn *had* found something that might help, she never saw Mouse anymore. Never heard from her. Everything seemed to be getting out of control lately. It had been a mistake, a terrible mistake, to throw the eye into the creek, as Mouse had done. And yet . . .

Judith came back in the kitchen. "Kenny and I are going to a movie at six. I hope Mom and Dad are back by then."

"Don't worry. I'll watch Stevie if they're not," Lynn said.

Judith sat down across from her and rested her elbows on the table. "Lynn, what's wrong?"

Lynn swallowed. "Everything."

"What's happened with Mouse?"

"She's . . . going around with some other girls."

Judith continued to study her, and Lynn felt tears welling up in her eyes.

"Going around with other girls and not including you?" Judith said. "Lynn, you and Mouse have been friends forever!"

It was too much. Lynn put her hands over her face and wept silently, nodding her head.

"*Tell* me," said Judith. "Tell me everything."

Tipping back her head, Lynn waited for the tears to stop, then dried her eyes with her napkin. She had to chance it. Dr. Long was out of town, and she had to talk with someone.

"Judith," she said, sniffling, "do you remember . . . a while back . . . when we were talking about Mrs. Tuggle, and you said if I ever needed you, to let you know because you didn't think you could fall under her power so easily again?"

"Yes . . ."

"I need you."

Judith's eyes widened. "This has something to do with *her*?"

Taking a deep breath, Lynn started at the beginning and told her sister everything. Judith listened intently, her lips slightly parted, not interrupting once.

"And now . . . that Mouse has joined their coven . . . I don't know of anything I can do to protect her," Lynn finished. "All this trouble is coming from the eye, Judith. I know it."

Judith sat shaking her head, dumbfounded. "My *gosh*, Lynn! And you've been keeping all this to yourself?"

"Before, I had Mouse to talk to. Now I don't even have her."

There was silence. Then: "You have me," said Judith determinedly.

"Do you really mean that?"

"I mean that I believe everything you've told me. Truly. With all my heart. Because I was under Mrs. Tuggle's spell too. You know what we've got to do, don't you?"

"Wh-what?"

"Find the eye."

"*What?*"

"The first chance we get, we'll . . ." Judith stopped because there was the sound of Father's car coming into the driveway. "They're home."

"*Tell* me," Lynn begged. "How are we going to find it?"

"Go wading," Judith said.

There was laughter from outside, and then Mr. and

Mrs. Morley entered the front door and came on out to the kitchen.

"I'm even worse than I thought, girls," Mother said gaily. "I think your father was ashamed to be seen with me."

Father chuckled as he put his golf clubs in the corner. "Not true! She's just a little rusty, that's all. Needs a lot more practice, and I'm going to see that she gets it. The exercise was good for you, Sylvia."

"It *is*, Mom. Your cheeks are as pink as your shirt!" said Judith. "I'm glad you had a good time. Lynn and I are about to go outside ourselves. I took Stevie to the park this morning, and wore him out. He's asleep on the glider."

"Thanks, sweetie," said her mother. "I guess I *did* need a day out. I'm feeling relaxed and wonderful."

The girls went quietly across the back porch so as not to waken Stevie, through the gate, then headed over the field. The purple-hooded plants on which Lynn had sprinkled salt were uglier still. She walked right over them on her way to the creek, and they clung to her shoes, as though trying to pull them off.

"That *smell*!" said Judith, looking around her. "It's like Mrs. Tuggle was right here, Lynn. Listen. Is that the *flowers* making that noise?"

Lynn nodded.

Judith shivered. "It's so creepy!" She went to the edge of the bank. "Now look, Lynn. Show me, as

nearly as you can, where you and Mouse were standing when she threw the eye."

Lynn tried to gauge it. Tried to remember how far they were from the footbridge and at what angle they had entered the creek.

"So you were about here," Judith guessed, wading into the water, "and Mouse was facing this way?"

Lynn demonstrated as best she could.

Judith reached down into the water and picked up a pebble about the size of a marble. "Throw it, Lynn, as hard as you can, and we'll see where it lands."

Lynn threw, and the stone went about fifteen yards downstream. They made a mental note of where it landed.

"Do it again," said Judith, fishing out another pebble.

Lynn threw once more. The stone landed near the place the other had, but hit a rock in midstream and bounced some distance away.

"See?" said Lynn in discouragement. "See all the things that could have happened to it? That eye, even if it is still around here, could be anywhere."

Nevertheless, she and Judith waded over to the place where the first stone had landed. The water came halfway up their legs, lapping gently at their knees. It was clear—clear enough to see much of the bottom, anyway—and the girls stooped low, picking up pebbles here and there, kicking others with their feet. The crows in the trees called raucously and the gulls in the sky screeched back.

Judith took one side of the creek, Lynn the other, and they waded down as far as they thought the eye might have traveled, then worked their way back up, using their feet to feel for anything small and round. But Lynn knew that the task was hopeless. Even if the eye was there after all this time, it could be embedded in the creek bank, buried in the mud, caught in the roots of a tree, impossible to see or find. More than likely the eye was gone, somewhere between here and New Orleans.

After a half hour, the girls gave up, climbed out, and wiped off their feet. The gaslike, perfumy scent of the flowers was even stronger now than before, and the one nearest Lynn seemed to hiss at her as she tied her sneakers. Angrily, Lynn hissed back, kicking at it with her foot. Almost immediately, all the flowers began to hum, louder and louder, higher and higher.

Judith covered her mouth, staring about her. "They're *horrible*, Lynn!"

In fury, Lynn stomped on the flower, trampling it with her foot until the stem was broken. The other salt-sprinkled flowers hushed but waved menacingly as though whispering, plotting, with each other.

"I'll get some more weed killer and take care of the ones that are left," Lynn told her sister. "Let's go home."

"From the shadows of the pool . . ." a wavery voice began.

Lynn looked quickly about her.

"Who is *that*?" Judith asked.

"Black as midnight, thick as gruel . . ."

The song, however, came from the flowers.

"Come, my nymphs, and you shall be, silent images of me."

"Ignore it, Judith. Just forget it."

"But that's the song Mrs. Tuggle taught me. I remember now. That first spring, when I was catching tadpoles in the creek. I'd sing that song and they'd swim right over to me, right into my hands. Oh, Lynn, I'm scared."

Lynn grabbed Judith by the shoulders. "We can't be scared. We can't *afford* to be scared off, Judith. I just ignore it. I just don't let it get to me, that's all. Come on, let's go home."

And then, as she started back up the path, Lynn made a terrible discovery. The flowers on which she had used the weed killer had seemed, from all appearances, dead—wilted and limp and pale—but when Lynn looked closely, she saw that they had sent out creepers—long, tubular roots that stretched stealthily across the ground for some distance, and beyond the place where the weed killer had fallen, small new flowers were springing up from the creepers, their tiny purple hoods poised like snakes, ready to strike.

chapter eleven

Things seemed hopeless. As the girls started home, Lynn thought about all that had happened since Judith met Mrs. Tuggle—the night Judith had tried to put Stevie out on the porch at midnight for the witches, the time Lynn and Mouse were alone at the Beasleys' and hundreds of cats and crows tried to get inside, the night she found Stevie carrying the eye. How many other horrible things would happen before they were rid of the evil once and for all? Or would they be? Ever?

Judith was the first one to speak. "What are you worried about most, Lynn? That the flowers will creep up to our house? That those girls will do something awful?"

"Mouse. I'm worried about her."

Judith chewed on one fingernail. "Listen, why don't I tell Kenny about this whole thing? He could get a bunch of guys together, and the next time the girls meet down by the water, he could go down and break it up."

"No!" Lynn grabbed her sister's arm and stopped

her. "Judith! *Promise* me you won't tell Kenny or *any-*
one outside our family!"

"Why?"

"Because at least the girls are meeting outside
where we can keep an eye on them. If Kenny broke
up their meetings, they'd just meet somewhere else—
in someone's basement, maybe, and then we'd never
know what's going on."

Judith didn't answer.

"Judith, listen to me. Kenny wouldn't believe this.
Couldn't believe it. He'd try to understand, but deep
down . . . You know how ridiculous all this sounds
to anyone else. It would leak out somehow, get to the
newspapers, and the whole town would think our
family's crazy. Please!"

Judith walked on slowly. "I'll think about it," she
said at last.

"No!" Lynn blocked her path. "Judith, this is serious. You've got to promise not to tell anyone else. I
can't stand it—I really can't—if on top of all this, I've
got to worry about you telling Kenny."

Judith put her arm around Lynn. "Okay, I promise.
You're right. It would only be an adventure to him."
There were tears in her eyes, Lynn noticed. "I wish
all this had never happened. I wish Mrs. Tuggle had
never come here, and I'd never gone to her house."
Her voice trembled just a little. "If it hadn't been for
me going up there to sew, our family never would
have been mixed up in it."

"How were you supposed to know, Judith? And if it wasn't you and our family, it would have been someone else."

"Just the same, I wish . . ."

"I know. I wish it every day. That I could just wake up some morning and discover it's all a nightmare, nothing more."

"Why don't we both go to Dad? Why don't we both sit down with him and maybe then he'll listen."

"It would be even better if Mouse was with us. Let me try to get her back, and then all three of us can go talk to Dad, and after that we'll go talk to Mr. Beasley. That's a good idea, Judith. They'd listen to all of us, I'll bet."

Judith left a little before six to meet Kenny at the theater, and Mr. Morley said he would make hamburgers on the grill outdoors. Lynn tried to be helpful. She put mustard and catsup on a tray and carried paper plates to the picnic table in the backyard.

"Lynn?" called her mother from the doorway. "Have you any idea what's happened to the salt? There's none in the shaker, and I can't find the box in the cupboard. I *know* I had a full box here somewhere."

Lynn could feel her cheeks flush. She tried to think of an excuse, but none came to mind. "I—I used it for an experiment," she said. "I meant to buy some more, but forgot. I'll ride down to the store right now and buy some."

"What kind of an experiment?" asked her father.

"I wanted to see if it would kill weeds."

Mr. Morley was looking at her strangely. "Whatever gave you that idea?"

"I was just fooling around," Lynn said defensively. "I didn't have anything else to do. Look, you don't have to make a federal case out of it. By the time the hamburgers are done, I'll be back with the salt."

She ran upstairs, got money out of her box, then rode to the store and was home in time to take her place at the picnic table.

That evening she was sitting out on the front steps with her transistor radio when Mother came out and sat beside her. For a moment Lynn went on listening, hoping that Mother had just come to enjoy the breeze and would go back in again, but then Mrs. Morley said, "Let's go for a walk, Lynn. Just you and me."

Lynn reluctantly turned her radio off. "Okay, where do you want to go?"

"Oh, anywhere. Up the hill for a change, maybe."

It was almost dark, and the first stars were out. Ordinarily Mouse would be spending the night over here or Lynn would be at the Beasleys'. At the very least, the girls would be together until ten or so before one of them went home.

"Lynn," Mother said when they had gone up the brick sidewalk only a short distance, "maybe you don't want to talk about it, but what's happened between you and Marjorie?"

"She's just busy, Mom, that's all."

"Sure?"

"She's got other friends."

"And you're not one of them?"

"Look. I really don't want to talk about it. Okay?"

"Okay."

Why couldn't she tell her mother? Lynn wondered, but she knew. Because she wasn't all that sure of Mother yet. If she told her what had really happened with Mouse, she'd have to tell her more. And if she told her more, she'd have to tell her everything. She wasn't sure that her mother was up to all that yet, and didn't dare take that chance.

"I remember when I was about your age," Mother went on. "I had a best friend, and there was a time she started liking another girl better than me. It was *so* hard, and I . . ." Mother went on talking, telling the story, and it made Lynn feel as though she were carrying a rock in the pit of her stomach. Mother thought it was just a problem of "best friends"— thought that she was helping, and Lynn loved her for it. But she wasn't helping at all, and there was no way Lynn could tell her that.

"Oh, look!" Mother stopped when they reached the top of the hill and had passed the tall trees that stood like sentinels between the sidewalk and the property beyond. "The house. It's almost done."

Lynn stared silently at the silhouette of the new house, built over the ashes of Mrs. Tuggle's old one. A thorn apple tree hid the front door completely from view, but she could see the rest of the house in the growing darkness. It stood out starkly against the purple sky, its turrets and gables fancier and more numerous than those of any other house on the street.

"It looks just like the old one," Lynn said. "Why would anybody want to build a house exactly like the one that had burned down? And in the very same spot?"

"Well, it *was* an authentic Victorian," Mother said. "And it *did* fit the landscape very well up here. All the houses on our street are Victorian, but Mrs. Tuggle's was always the grandest. I guess the new owners want to keep the same architecture as the rest of the neighborhood."

They walked down a side street, then turned again, came down past the school, and turned toward home.

"Marjorie will miss you after a while, Lynn," Mother said. "I promise. She'll be back."

"Oh, Mom . . ." Lynn said, swallowing. She could say no more, and went on up to her room.

It was on Sunday, however, that she got the hard questions.

"Lynn!"

She had been writing in her journal about telling Judith everything, about going to the creek with her sister to try and find the eye, when her father's voice yelled to her from downstairs.

Lynn went out in the hall. "Yes?"

"Come down here."

Still thinking he needed her for something, she clattered on down to the first floor. Mr. Morley was frowning. "Come out here," he said, and she followed him outside. Then she knew.

"What happened to all my weed killer? Did you use that too?"

Lynn stared at the ground, nodding. She could feel her father's eyes on her without even looking.

"Lynn, what the heck has got into you? Is this some more of that witchcraft nonsense?"

She managed to look up. "I don't know what it is. But Mouse is mixed up with those girls now, and I wanted to help."

"*What* girls?"

"Some girls who have started a witches' coven. They've been meeting in those purple flowers—those weeds—down by the creek, and I know it's the weeds that are doing it—luring them there. I couldn't think of what else to do except try to kill the weeds."

"Lynn, this is just incredible!" Her father's face showed both exasperation and despair.

"I know." Lynn felt the same way.

"I don't know whether to believe you, to punish you . . ."

"I'm sorry I used all the weed killer, Dad. I was going to ask for an advance on next week's allowance and buy some more."

"None of this makes any sense. It just doesn't connect. Are there things you haven't told me?"

"Lots."

"Why not?"

"Because you won't believe me."

"Have you told them to Dr. Long?"

"Yes. I saw him the other day."

"And did you tell him everything?"

Lynn nodded.

"Does he believe you?"

"I don't know. He said he'd keep an open mind."

There was silence for a while, and when Lynn looked at her father again, he was studying her with concern. Finally he went over and sat down on the concrete steps that led to the cellar from outside. "Sit down here, Lynn," he said.

She did.

"If I promise the same thing, will you tell everything to me?"

Her heart pounded. "Yes."

"Okay," he said, his face serious. "Let's hear it all."

Lynn could not help wishing Judith were there to back her up, give her courage. But just as she had done with her sister, Lynn started at the point where Mrs. Tuggle's house had burned to the ground and Stevie had found the glass eye. She told him about the night the bat had got into the house, singing Mrs. Tuggle's songs, and how Lynn had followed it hypnotically to the creek where, to save her, Mouse had pulled the eye from Lynn's pajama pocket and tossed it out into the swirling water. She explained about the strange appearance of the purple-hooded flowers shortly afterward, and how some of the girls from school, who played down there on the creek bank, had formed the Coventry Club, drugged Lynn with one of the flowers, and taken Mouse into their coven. When she had finished at last, trying the best she could to stick to facts as she knew them, she glanced at her father. He was resting his head in his hands.

There was silence in the yard except for a bee, a breeze, Stevie's voice from somewhere upstairs, the clatter of dishes in the kitchen. But finally her father spoke:

"If I had to give up everything—our house, my job, our money—to see you free of this, Lynn, I would. It's worth that much to me."

"But you've already done a lot, Dad—buying that book from Mr. Beasley for two thousand dollars so the girls couldn't get it." She had promised to tell him everything, so she had to let him know that she knew about this, too.

"Two thousand *dollars?*" He turned toward her.

"I know about that book you bought from Mr. Beasley, Dad. I found it yesterday when I was dusting under your bed. I feel terrible that you had to spend so much to get it."

Mr. Morley smiled wanly. "One dollar, Lynn, that's

all I paid for it. Marjorie's father was alarmed at all the attention that book has been getting, and asked me to buy it from him for a dollar so he could honestly say it had been sold. Later, I'll sell it back to him."

Lynn was relieved. "Don't sell it anytime soon, Dad. If Betty or Charlotte Ann or Kirsten . . ."

"It stays here," he answered. "In the meantime, Lynn, will you continue to see Dr. Long? I'll feel a great deal better if I know another adult is listening to this too and can help make heads or tails of it."

"I'm going to see him tomorrow."

"Good. And do I have your permission to ask him from time to time how things are going?"

"He can tell you anything, Dad. Do you still think it's all in my head?"

"No. Not all. But how much is true and how much you only perceive to be true, I don't know. Mr. Beasley's as concerned as I am. There are too many things we don't understand, and we don't seem to be getting very far."

Lynn almost began to feel hopeful. "Mr. Beasley's worried about Mouse?"

"He says she's been staying in her room a lot."

"Then you *will* talk to him, Dad? Will you tell him about the witches' coven and how the girls got her to join? That *I'm* worried?"

"I'll try to talk to him this next week, Lynn. I can't

tell him it's a witches' coven, because I have no real proof of that, but I *can* say that you're worried."

"Tell him that *I* think it's a witches' coven, then. Whatever it is, Dad, he ought to be worried about Mouse. If those girls *are* killing birds and things, I know he wouldn't want Mouse hanging around with them. Someone should stop them. Please tell him that. He'll listen to you."

"Okay, Lynn, I will," her father said, and, as he stood up to go inside, added, "By the way, I would really prefer that your mother not know any of this."

"I wasn't planning to tell her," Lynn said. "Not yet, anyway."

Later, when Judith came in, Lynn said, "I told him."

Judith paused in the doorway of their room. "Dad? You *told* him?"

Lynn nodded and put down her journal. "Everything."

"What did he say?" Judith came over slowly and sat down on the foot of Lynn's bed.

"He was mad because I'd used all the weed killer, so I had to tell him. He said . . . if he had to give up everything—our house, his job—to get me free of all this, he would."

"Our *house*! His *job*!" Judith repeated anxiously.

"He just wanted me to know how worried he is."

"Then he believes!"

"Not entirely."

Judith sighed and her shoulders slumped. "I wish we could talk to Mother about it. I wish we could just all sit down as a family, talk about all that's happened, what we remember. . . ."

"So do I, Judith. So do I."

There was one bit of comfort, however. The next day, as soon as Lynn had finished sitting Stevie while Mother wrote, she excused herself early from lunch and went back upstairs to read more of *Spells and Potions*. If the eye was never found, would it go on affecting them forever and ever? When she had been reading the book on Saturday—about how a witch's ashes should be scattered to the winds—Lynn seemed to remember reading something else that she had hurried over at the time. But now it seemed important to read it again.

Quietly she got the book out from under her parents' bed, took it up to her own room, and found the page once again:

> *Should a witch meet her death by fire, her ashes are to be scattered to the winds; otherwise one cannot be certain that her power is extinguished. If, however, any part of her remains, that portion cannot contain the evil for long, for the power of evil is such that it shall, in time, infect its surroundings, and that part of the witch that was unconsumed by fire would of itself lose its power, the evil moving on. . . .*

Lynn leaned back against the wall. If this were true, then the eye, wherever it was, or whether it still existed at all, could no longer hurt them, was no longer, in itself, a threat. And if Lynn's hunch was true, the evil that the eye had left behind—in spores, in seeds, or water—was now in the purple-hooded flowers on the bank. It did not make her less afraid of the flowers; it only helped to know that the evil was contained in one place.

At three, she rode over to the school and went down the hall to Dr. Long's conference room. There was a CONFERENCE IN SESSION sign on the door, so Lynn sat on the bench outside. Fifteen minutes later, a couple came out and left. Dr. Long was about to close the door again when he saw Lynn.

"You came about the flower?" he asked.

"Yes. Is this a good time?"

Dr. Long was unsmiling, and Lynn had the uneasy feeling that he didn't really want to see her. "Come on in," he said. "I have only a few minutes now, but we'll make another appointment when we can talk longer."

She went inside and sat down, waiting.

"I don't know if what I found out is going to help matters any or make them worse," he said. "But in our first session together, Lynn, you promised to level with me, so I'm going to be straightforward with you. I took the flower over to the horticulture department at the university as I said I would. They were frankly puzzled. The professor called in some colleagues, and they all agreed it was a plant they had never seen before. After examining it for some time, however, they finally decided that it's a member of the figwort family, and its botanical name is *Scrophulariaceae.*" He paused. "It's commonly known as witchweed."

Lynn didn't move. *Couldn't.*

"Even though the common type of witchweed has red or yellow flowers, not purple, they tell me it has the same characteristics. Witchweed is a sort of parasitic plant, growing on the roots of corn and some kinds of grasses. It has tiny seeds that are spread by the wind. It also lives for many, many years."

Lynn said what she knew he was thinking. What her father would say if he were here. "Do you think it's just a coincidence that it's called witchweed?"

Dr. Long didn't look at her. Just sat with fingers folded on his chest, tapping his chin with one forefinger. "It could be coincidence, of course. But I have to tell you something else. I asked the professors if they could tell me what, short of burning the plant, we might do to get rid of it. They said if I would leave it overnight, they'd have some time the next day to try various chemicals on it and see. The strange part— the really strange part—is that when they went back to test the flower the next morning, it had turned to dust. Just crumbled like ashes, and there was nothing left."

*

A public hearing had been called for August 1, the next evening, on the need for a recreation center. While Lynn entertained Stevie, Mother had been on the phone all morning asking people to go and show their support. As soon as Father got home from work, he took over the phone.

Mr. Beasley came by to ride over to the high school auditorium with Lynn's parents. When he saw Lynn, he said, "Haven't seen you around much lately, Lynn. I've missed you at the bookshop. Hope you and Marjorie haven't had a falling out. I can't get very much out of her."

"I'm not mad at *her*," Lynn said in answer. She glanced at her father. *Tell him*, her eyes begged, and she knew that he would.

After they had gone, she sat on the porch, leaning against a post and watching the moon, a full moon. The moon had driven Judith and Kenny together; they had headed off toward the park, arms around each other, each with a hand in the hip pocket of the other's jeans, which Lynn thought perfectly ridiculous. But they had taken Stevie with them, and he was excited about being out at night. They had invited Lynn, too, but she hadn't wanted to come. She didn't want to do anything lately but think, and the more she thought, the worse things seemed.

A cool front was moving in, and Lynn shivered as she felt the breeze. It occurred to her suddenly that this was one of the dates of a witches' Sabbat, and that, plus the pale moon making shadows on the sidewalk, brought the goose bumps out on her arms. She stared up at the moon, trying to make out all the little dark spots and ridges, hypnotized almost by that huge bone-white eye in the sky, when she realized that the phone was ringing.

She walked inside and answered.

"Lynn," came a frightened, faraway voice. *"Help me."*

chapter twelve

Mouse.

"Where are you?" Lynn asked. "What's wrong?"

"I'm at home." The voice was only a whisper. "Nothing's happened yet, but it's going to. Lynn, I'm so scared!"

"Why? Should I come over?"

"You can't. *They're* here."

"Where?"

"Out on the porch. They'd stop you."

"Then you sneak out the back and come over here."

"Lynn, I t-tried, but there are birds all over the back porch. Crows, gulls, blackbirds, jays . . ."

Trapped.

"Stay inside then, and I'll get help."

"It might be too late. They're celebrating Lammas tonight."

"Lammas?"

"One of the Sabbats. Betty is going to get her highest powers tonight, and they're going to make me an official member of the coven. Listen. Can you hear them?"

There was the sound of Mouse moving across the

floor with the telephone, and then, dimly, Lynn could
hear the other girls chanting out on the Beasleys'
front porch:

> Sing of morning, sing of noon,
> Sing of evening's silver moon.
> Feel the darkness, touch the black,
> Hear the shadows whisper back.

One of Mrs. Tuggle's old songs! Lynn shuddered.
"Mouse, don't go with them. Promise me you won't!"

"They'll be in to get me pretty soon. I told them I
couldn't go anywhere until I did the dishes, and I said
I wasn't allowed to have anyone in when Dad's not
here. They'll wait for a while, but not very long. Oh,
Lynn . . ." Mouse's voice broke. "It's going to be awful! The ceremony has to take place by water, so it's
going to be down by the creek among the purple flowers, and Betty's going to k-kill Oliver." Mouse was
sobbing now.

"Wh-who?"

"Oliver—her pet rat. They s-said that for a witch to
attain her full powers, she has to sacrifice her familiar, so she's going to sacrifice Oliver."

Lynn gasped.

"I can't stand this, Lynn!" Mouse wept. "I don't care
whether I can get the power to bring Mom back or
not. I don't want anything else to die. I want out."

Those were the words Lynn had been wanting to

hear all weekend, yet still her knees were shaking. "Mouse," she said. "Stay where you are, and don't go with them. Make excuses. Take a long time with the dishes. Get sick. Throw up, if you have to."

"What if they come in and try to drag me out?"

"Listen, Mouse. Do you still have ashes in your fireplace?"

"We *always* have ashes in our fireplace."

"Go get some and make a circle around yourself in the kitchen. Stay inside that circle. Do it *now*, Mouse —as soon as you hang up. I'll think of something."

Her fingers were trembling as she hung up the phone. Her first thought was to call Mr. Beasley, but he was with the others at the high school across town. Even if she called the high school, there would be no one in the office at this hour to answer the phone.

She ran upstairs and found Dr. Long's card with his phone number on it, came back down and dialed his home. One ring, two, three . . .

"Hello? Longs' residence."

"This is Lynn Morley. Is Dr. Long there? I've got to speak to him."

"I'm sorry, but he went to the hearing at the high school. He won't be back until ten or eleven. This is Mrs. Long. Is there a message?"

Lynn closed her eyes and swallowed. "No . . . it'll be too late," she said, and hung up.

Through the window she could see the moon, pale

and ghostlike, riding high in the sky. . . . Should she call the police? And tell them what? That a group of girls was sitting on somebody's porch, trapping that somebody inside, and she couldn't come out the back door because some birds were out there? Lynn would be taken to the hospital for observation.

And suddenly she knew what she had to do. She would not only be saving Mouse but a little white rat as well. If the ceremony had to take place on a Sabbat, then it had to be tonight or not at all this summer.

She did not think twice, did not worry about what her parents might say. She took matches from the kitchen, ran outside to the tool shed, and picked up the can of gasoline her father used for the mower, then out the garden gate and across the meadow.

And the witchweed knew. The hum grew louder with every step she took. The sky was not quite dark, yet everything appeared in shadow, and overhead, the large dry eye of a moon stared down at her.

The hum was deafening as she neared the footbridge, and when she took her first step among the purple-hooded flowers, the hum turned to a buzz, and then, out of that eerie cacophony of noise, words:

> Sing of morning, sing of noon,
> Sing of evening's silver moon.
> Feel the darkness, touch the black,
> Hear the shadows whisper back.

Lynn unscrewed the lid of the gasoline. Slowly she lifted the can and began moving around the perimeter of the purple-hooded flowers, pouring a thin stream as she went. The witchweed seemed to have become fingers, scratching at her ankles, clutching at her socks.

Grasshoppers and other insects also seemed to know what Lynn was about to do. The field was suddenly alive with them, all leaping away—flocks of them, herds of them, swarms of grasshoppers—deserting the field.

The temperature was dropping, and on the surface of Cowden's Creek a fog had begun to gather. Lynn went on, pulling her feet up out of the witchweed. Once more the hum became a buzz, and the buzz became words—a hissing, whispery sort of incantation:

> Fast upon us, spirits all,
> Listen for our whispered call.
> Whistling kettle, tinkling bell,
> Weave your web, and spin your spell.

The fog was forming itself once again into a hand. A single finger bent and beckoned, but Lynn paid it no attention. In the evening sky, she could make out one crow circling, then two, then three, as though they had been called. She moved hurriedly. When she had surrounded the entire patch of witchweed with gasoline, she crisscrossed the center of it, pouring another trail, her ankles bleeding with the pricks and scratches the plants had made.

The misty hand was hovering now just above the bank, its long fingers curled and grasping. Lynn felt one dank finger of fog brush her cheek. She threw away the empty can and moved backward, distancing herself from the circle of gasoline. Then, wiping her fingers hard on the dew-covered grass, she carefully, carefully lit a match and, holding it far out in front of her, tossed it into the trail she had made.

The cold, damp fingers of fog curled around her throat, and for a moment Lynn couldn't breathe. It was the way it had been when Betty thrust the purple flower in her face. Lynn struggled, gasping, and then she saw the tongue of fire streak around the circle, and the hand released its grasp. On the fire went, weaving here, weaving there, until the witchweed was completely enclosed. A separate tongue flared out, crisscrossing the center. A cry filled the air—half scream, half shriek—whether from the birds or plants, Lynn didn't know, and the whole plot of witchweed went up in flames.

Taking the far path toward the Beasleys', Lynn ran as fast as she could. She knew that as soon as the girls got a whiff of the smoke, they would be over in a moment, and she wanted to be off the path when they came.

It didn't take long. She was almost through the grass and down to Mouse's street when she heard the thud of running feet, the voices and shouts of Betty and the other girls as they came pounding up the path. Lynn threw herself into the bushes on one side and lay as though she were dead until they passed. Then she picked herself up again and ran on, down the path, down the hill, across the street, and finally she was scrambling up the steps of the Beasleys' porch and pounding on the door. Mouse opened it, threw her arms around Lynn's neck, and began to sob.

"Oh, Lynn, it's been terrible! I didn't think they'd ever leave. I didn't think you'd ever come!"

Lynn went inside and locked the door behind her. They collapsed on the deacon's bench in the hall. "Mouse," Lynn said, grabbing her friend's hands. "Are you okay?"

Marjorie seemed to have lost several pounds. There were dark circles under her eyes, as though she hadn't slept, and her skin was pale.

"Now that you're here, Lynn, I'm okay," she wept. "It's been awful without you. They said I couldn't talk to you or call you or come over or anything. If I did, it would break the spell, and I'd never get Mom home again. They called me Sevena, just like Mrs. Tuggle did, and they said that when I've reached my highest power, I could make spells that would send people away or bring people back. I wanted . . . I wanted to see if . . ." Her lips trembled.

"I know," said Lynn. "It's okay, Mouse. Really."

"But it was terrifying. Betty and Charlotte Ann—all of them—they're not like they used to be. It's the flowers, I know it. They worship those flowers. They wear them or carry them and pin them in their hair."

"It's witchweed," Lynn told her. "I gave one of the flowers to Dr. Long and he had it examined at the university."

"Oh, Lordy!" Mouse gasped.

"But it won't bother us again, Mouse. I've destroyed it."

"How?"

Lynn started to answer, then stopped, turning her head and listening. There was the sound of sirens off in the distance.

She leapt up and flung open the front door. She could see a red glow in the sky over the field. "Mouse!" she screamed.

And then the girls were running at breakneck speed, stumbling, sliding, clawing their way through the tangle of vines and bushes on the hillside, up the back path to the field. When they got to the top, Lynn stared.

The fire had spread all across the meadow. Flames were leaping up, dissolving into hot sparks that did a ritual dance in the darkness, then rained down on the embers below. They were heading toward the Morleys' and the other houses on the street. Already flames were licking at the fence at the back of the garden.

Lynn screamed and the dark row of bushes in front of her there in the field turned to stare in her direction, only they weren't bushes at all, she realized, but the five girls who had been sitting on Marjorie's porch. They looked at Lynn with dazed, expressionless eyes, their power gone. Lynn grabbed Mouse by the hand and ran on, just as the Morleys' back gate swung open, and the gray figures of firemen in their chunky helmets, boots, and coats lumbered through, dragging hoses behind them.

By the time the girls reached the garden, firemen were hosing down the fence, which was already charred at one end. Hoses were spread out all over the field. The firemen ran this way and that, calling to each other, and the thick black smoke from the burning weeds and grasses hung heavy over the meadow, mingling with the darkness and masking the moon.

Lynn started to sob. She could not believe that she had done such an incredibly stupid thing as to go off and leave a fire. There had been no rain for more than a week, the sun had been hot, and the field was dry. The fire could have burned up the Morleys' house and all the others on the block. She and Mouse clung to each other as they watched the fire recede, the red embers showering down, the dark silhouettes of firemen as they began to move more slowly now, to stop and catch their breath. Out on the street, the loud roar of the engines went on.

And then someone else ran through the back gate, stopped, looked around, and ran toward Lynn. It was Mr. Morley, followed by Dr. Long.

For a moment they said nothing, Lynn and her father. Just hugged. She wanted to stay in those strong arms forever, forget all that had happened. She felt the tears again.

"Dad," she wept. "I had to save Mouse, and burning was the only way to stop the evil."

The strong arms squeezed her tightly. She smelled the comforting scent of his aftershave, his skin.

"You're safe," he said. "You're both safe. That's what matters. I believe you, Lynn. Let's go home."

He put one arm around Lynn, the other around Mouse, and herded them back over the field, across the tangle of hoses and on toward the gate where Dr. Long, and now Mr. Beasley, waited.

Would this be the end of it, then? Lynn wondered as she smelled the smoky ruin of the witchweed and grass. The sky had returned to gray again, and the sparks that had been showering down only a few minutes before were dull red embers beneath her feet.

Except for one. One *something*, anyway. Because far up the hill, where a new house was being built over the ashes of Mrs. Tuggle's old one, there was a gleam—a greenish yellow glow—like the moon caught off course, or a star expelled from the heavens. Lynn stared intently, but just as she was about to tell her dad, the light went out, and there was only darkness where the gleam had been.